Family Secrets

Family Secrets

LEE ANDERSON

AVALON BOOKS
THOMAS BOUREGY AND COMPANY, INC.
401 LAFAYETTE STREET
NEW YORK, NEW YORK 10003

ROM
F
AND

CHAPTER ONE

No one has ever complimented me for my patience, and I've rarely given anyone reason to. One day last April, while my true colors were flying high, I was alone in my office. I paced the floor, drummed my fingernails on the desk, and drank a week's ration of coffee.

I looked at my watch and inhaled deeply. I frowned at the phone. Jason had said he'd call me by four o'clock. It was four forty-five. I slumped into my desk chair and let out a long breath. I like to think I know when I'm overreacting or being childish or acting just plain dumb. I had a strong feeling I was doing all three, but it didn't help. This was hardly a life-and-death situation, I reminded myself.

When the opportunity to work at the Kincade ranch had arisen, I saw it as an exciting challenge. For my personal life the timing couldn't have been better. I'd just ended a romance I should have ended three months sooner. My lovely old apartment house was to be torn down to make room for a shopping mall. My best friend had eloped over the weekend, and two days before I'd weathered my twenty-sixth birthday. I needed a change.

Also, living in the country on a ranch with a big stable held a lot of charm. And on top of everything else I was very fond of Jason B. Kincade, Senior. I had tried to act interested, ready to cooperate, and confident that I could handle the job. What I had tried not to do was show how excited I was about the prospect of working at the ranch.

Jason Kincade, Junior, who had discussed the matter with me, had a low tolerance for emotional people. To him, emotional responses suggested instability. Any woman with anything but an icy-calm manner could send him scurrying to a forgotten appointment. At times it was comical, but it was also a fact of life and what I considered probably his only flaw. It was also amazing that I had been able to keep a cool exterior around him for over three years.

J.B., as Jason Kincade, Senior, was called, was his son's opposite. He enjoyed a heated discussion. He was volatile, and he expected others to be also. To him it was a sign they thought for themselves, paid attention, and were unintimidated. All admirable traits, he said. Around J.B. I had an easier time of it. Although it had caused me a little trouble at times, expressing my opinions had never been one of my life's problems. J.B. and I got along quite well.

After J.B. had a stroke, he couldn't accept the fact that he must stay away from the strain of his office for an extended period of time. Always a man to find a solution to any problem, he decided that a sophisticated computer system, linked to the various control centers of Kincade Industries, could be set up in a small room on the first floor of his home. A temporary bedroom could be set up for him next to this office. All the necessary software and copies of files for all phases of Kincade Industries' current projects could be transported to the ranch.

There was, however, one problem. J.B. needed someone who could chart data on projects in progress in the labs and someone who knew how to obtain the latest pertinent information from headquarters through the wonders of our computer network. It would have to be someone he knew, someone he liked, and someone he could work with in a degree of harmony. Insistence on the last part came from his doctor, who thoroughly disapproved of the whole project.

J.B.'s first choice was Roger Austin, longtime project coordinator for Kincade Industries. But Roger was too necessary to the operation of Kincade Industries for him to consider either moving to the ranch or the daily commute of fifty miles each way. Also, Roger had an invalid wife. At the office he was only ten minutes away from her. He didn't want to increase that distance, and J.B. understood.

During my three years with Kincade Industries I had the good fortune to move up through the ranks with unprecedented speed. Some of it was pure luck, and part of it was timing. A lot of it was the fact that I could learn quickly and was willing to work very hard without one eye on the clock.

Just before J.B.'s stroke I was made one of Roger Austin's assistants. Since J.B. knew me and we got along well and I had the expertise he needed, I became a logical second choice.

After J.B. and I had spent a long time on the phone, Jason sauntered into my office, trying to act as though he just happened to be in the neighborhood. I knew better. I'd seen him watching me while I talked to his father. He gave me a tight smile as he closed the door. "Laura, I want to be sure you know what you could be getting into if you accept this job with my father. You know it's voluntary. If you refuse, it won't in any way affect your standing with our company."

I nodded. "I know."

"My family can be very wearing." Jason's handsome face showed his concern as he hitched his leg over the corner of my desk and sat down.

"Thanks for your concern, Jason, but I'm sure I'd have no problem. I'm very fond of your father, and I worked closely with him on that Whitaker project. We got along fine. I learned the secret early. I either ignore him when he roars, or I roar back."

Jason narrowed his eyes. "I know. You can handle him better than most. But he can be very demanding. My mother and my sister can be trying at times too. You and Grandfather are great friends, he says, but he can be cantankerous. Then there's my cousin, Kyle Marklin. He's staying at the house now, helping Dad. You'll have to watch out for him."

I stood up and looked over at his great big beautiful

eyes. "Jason, I'd probably see little of your mother, sister, or cousin since they're not involved in the business. J.B. and your grandfather will keep me busy at the computer and with charts. You know how they love charts. Also, J.B. told me his horses will be at my disposal. They'll take care of my spare time. I love to ride."

Jason stood up, and his eyes smiled down at me. "Okay. I'll get back to you within a couple of hours. Uncle Harvey and I are going back out to the ranch to settle this once and for all. We're still very much against this whole idea. Dad needs rest. We're going to try once more to change his mind. I'll call you by"—he looked at his watch—"four o'clock." He grinned. "You're a brave lady to consider doing this, Laura Grant."

It was five-thirty when the phone rang. "Laura, Jason here."

"Yes, Jason." I cleared my throat and realized I had a death grip on the phone.

"Well, Dad and Gramps won again. They're going through with this office at the ranch, and you're the one they want out here. Are you absolutely sure you want to do this?"

I clamped my teeth together for a moment to keep from squealing for joy. "Yes, Jason, I'm sure. In fact, I'll enjoy the change of scenery for a while." I was proud of my even tone of voice.

"Okay, it's your choice. I'll try to get out here weekends and ride with you. There are some beautiful trails that are hard to find if you don't know about them."

"I'd like that." Oh, yes, I'd like that a lot! I often wondered if he had any idea about the crush I had on him. I didn't take it seriously, of course. I did know better than that. Just about every woman at Kincade Industries was half in love with him. Someone was always gushing over him. He handled it all very well, though. He had a way of acting as though he didn't notice. Some actor, our handsome prince.

Jason had called his sister *trying.* I considered Amanda a pain soon after I met her. She sauntered into my office on my second day at the ranch and asked me what color I used on my hair. "It's what Mother Nature used," I said.

"Really? One doesn't usually see such fair skin and such blue eyes with such black hair," she said, as though she knew what she was talking about.

"It all came as a package," I said as I juggled some files from a box.

"You should wear your hair longer. It's too severe, brushed back at the sides and so short in the back." She looked around at the myriad of papers on my desk. "Are you working on that Hardcase project everyone's so excited about?"

The question caught me by surprise. Hardcase was the code name for our most secret project. Few knew about it. I shrugged. "At the moment I'm hardly sure what I'm working on. We have so much data here that I haven't begun to sort it out." It was a boldfaced lie, but if J.B. wanted to talk to an airbrain like his daughter about our secret projects, he could. I wasn't about to tell anyone anything.

"I guess you wouldn't have time to address some envelopes for me, then?"

I shook my head no, and she left the office without further comment. Although we were close in age, I knew we had little in common. I hoped we'd get along.

The next time she barged into my office, I was standing by the file cabinet. She looked up at me. "How tall are you?"

"I'm five-seven. Why?"

"I wish I were that tall. I bet you really have to work at it to stay so slim all the time. I'm going to leave this list of addresses and these envelopes here on your desk. They need to be addressed very neatly. I don't need them until Thursday. Let me know when you're finished with them."

I picked up her little packet and held it out to her. "Sorry, Amanda. I work for your father, but I'll talk to him about hiring a secretary for you."

She glared at me, grabbed her envelopes and list, and stomped out of the office. "Don't bother," she said over her shoulder.

That scene set the tone for our relationship, which promised to be tenuous at best.

Jason's mother, Emily, appeared rather confused most of the time and vague about most everything. In a conversation with her, it was often difficult to decide whether you were both discussing the same subject. But she was a delightful person who breezed around the house, talking to her constant companion, a small white poodle named Daisy.

Kyle Marklin, J.B.'s nephew, was the other family member Jason had warned me about. At our first meeting I felt Kyle was secure with the idea that he was the world's gift to women. I knew the type well and worked at avoiding him.

Grandfather Kincade, or Gramps as he told me to call him, was a delightful old man nearing eighty-two. He was full of vinegar even though confined to a wheelchair. He was kept under a degree of control by a large robust nurse he referred to as Rambo. Her name was Marie Trent. She was on to all of Gramps's tricks and bickered with him constantly. They adored each other, but both would go to the wall before they'd say a good word to or about the other.

The two dogs, who closely resembled wolves and guarded the ranch house with the zeal of hungry lions, scared me half to death the day I arrived at the ranch to stay. They sniffed at my heels while low threatening sounds came from deep in their chests. Kyle told me I'd be all right as long as I didn't make any sudden moves. There was no fear of that. I was paralyzed.

"They'll accept you when they know you live here," Kyle said.

They followed Kyle and me to my room, sniffed me and my luggage, and then pushed against my thighs for a pet. To the inhabitants of the house, they were pets. To anyone they didn't know, those two were a menacing pair that liked to show their long fangs against a background of terrorizing growls. It was proudly said the dogs could hear a pin drop on the carpet or on the lawn.

Such was the group I had elected to live with for the next three or four months. There were drawbacks, of course. For one thing, the ranch was ten miles from the nearest small town, and it was fifty miles from Sacramento. Emily, J.B.'s wife, insisted I was to feel I was a part of the family. I wasn't sure I wanted to, but I knew I'd work it out.

I felt Amanda and Kyle were both odd, but I wasn't sure why I felt that way. And then there were those lengthy phone calls that J.B. placed every afternoon and that left him testy and short-tempered. Those moods could last for quite some time. But, of course, I knew he was temperamental. I often opted to take my meals in the kitchen with Mrs. Kiley, the housekeeper. It was more fun.

Although everyone at the Kincade ranch was not lovable at all times, they all did appear harmless enough. I didn't doubt I'd love living at the ranch, at least for a while. I'd better like it, I told myself as I unpacked. I had no place else to live. Most of my things were in storage, and I'd placed a large deposit on a new apartment that wouldn't be ready for at least ninety days.

By the fourth Saturday of my stay at the ranch I felt I knew everyone fairly well. J.B. and I had had our share of crisp words. He often expected instant miracles from me. I pointed out to him quite often that I was one person and not a complete office staff. He was getting better about his expectations, but he still had a way to go. That day started out sanely enough.

Amanda's latest boyfriend, Ralph Satterly, who worked in accounting at Kincade Industries, showed up early. Ralph was much too agreeable and smiled too much for my liking. J.B. watched him walk across the terrace and spoke without looking at me. "It's comforting to know he won't last long. Amanda changes boyfriends as often as she changes the color of her hair." I knew Ralph's days were numbered.

Harvey Kincade, J.B.'s younger brother, who was more or less at the head of Kincade Industries during J.B.'s absence, arrived just behind Ralph with data for J.B.'s approval. Harvey had a certain amount of expertise in the field of finance and contract negotiations, but his illusions of adequacy in every field often caused tension within the firm. He was a man in love with details. J.B. had no patience with detail. He cared only about progress reports, comparison charts, and the end products. The two men didn't always get along. That morning they started arguing right after they said hello.

I escaped to the kitchen to have a cup of coffee with Mrs. Kiley. Along with Marie Trent, she had become my haven when the frequent family storms began to brew. She started talking as soon as she saw me. "As you know, today is Gramps's birthday, and he's insisting everyone show up at brunch. It's a rarity around here. The women are always dieting, and they hate to see how the men eat."

The big woman filled my coffee cup and placed a fresh hot blueberry muffin on a plate in front of me. "If I eat your cooking much longer, I'll have to diet too," I told her.

Mrs. Kiley's shoulders shook in laughter. "I'm trying to fill you out. You need it, you know. Oh, by the way, Jason called early this morning and said he wouldn't be here in time to go riding before brunch." The gray-haired woman grinned mischievously. "Now tell me—is there something kind of serious between you and young Jason?"

I felt the heat rise in my face. "Not at all."

She gave me a knowing grin. "He's been around a lot more than usual lately." She narrowed her eyes. "I think we'd better keep an eye on this."

I set my cup down. "Now, Mrs. Kiley, don't let your imagination run away with you. Jason and I have worked together a lot and he's—"

Mrs. Kiley cut me off. "He told me he comes out so often because of his father's condition. I told him that sounded good to me if that's the excuse he's going to use." She chuckled.

"Jason works very hard," I said flatly. "He's a man who takes his work seriously." It was true. Even those who resented nepotism admitted that Jason was smart and would be able to handle everything on his own someday.

Mrs. Kiley gave me a knowing grin and, thankfully, changed the subject. "You know, I dreamed about Michael again last night. It's the third night in a row. I usually do that just about the time he shows up."

"Ah, you're a psychic. Who's Michael?"

"That boy's been on my mind a lot lately. And then he called Gramps last night. No one in the family's to know, by the way. He's the oldest of these kids." She shook her head. "He takes off without telling anyone where he's going or what he's going to do. It drives everyone nuts. He calls every couple of months, though, to make sure everyone is okay. Then he'll send a Christmas card from France and maybe a postcard from Cairo, with no explanation about what he's doing there. Then, out of the blue, he shows up on the doorstep. Everyone's usually miffed at him for not letting them in on his secret life." She shrugged. "He's a love, that boy, and has been since the day he was born. Wish he'd stay around more. He'd keep this place hopping."

"He's not interested in Kincade Industries, I gather."

She shook her head. "Nope. He's more the adventurous type. He says Jason can keep the family happy for both of them."

"How old is Michael?"

"He's thirty-four now, I think. He's two years older than Jason."

I liked the tidbits Mrs. Kiley dropped about everyone. The woman didn't have a malicious bone in her body, but she wasn't above calling things as she saw them. I liked it, too, that she trusted me as she did.

My curiosity was aroused about Michael, and I wondered why I'd never heard of him before. I'd also wondered about Kyle lately. He'd been acting a little weird, I thought. "Does Kyle live here most of the time?"

"Kyle's a freeloader. He lives here for a while, then he goes home for a while, and then he drops out of sight for a while. His mother, who's dead now, was J.B.'s sister. I'll have to admit, he's been a help in getting J.B. up in the morning, getting him showered and dressed, and getting him ready for bed at night. J.B.'s such a big man. I'm not sure how we'd have managed without Kyle. He's a good kid. Just shiftless, I guess."

I'd kept my distance from Kyle Marklin even though he was attractive and continually invited me to accompany him on walks and for dinner and a show in town. I'd told him I was too tired so often, he probably wondered about my general health. It did annoy me that I'd found him sitting on my desk, glancing at the papers scattered around, three times in one week when I returned from lunch. I started locking everything in my desk anytime I left the office. And that annoyed me too.

The first occurrence that shook up the family that day happened while we were having brunch. It was warmer than usual for that time of year, and everyone was seated at a big circular table on the terrace. Jason slid into the chair beside me. His smile was captivating. Without a suit coat and tie, with his shirt opened at the neck and his sleeves rolled up just above his wrists, he gave off a totally different aura than his buttoned-down look at the office. He was handsome either way, but I preferred this more casual image few at the office ever saw.

We had become good friends through the past weeks, but I had no illusions that it would turn into anything more. Although he worked to make it appear that his life totally revolved around Kincade Industries, I didn't buy it for a minute. In fact, I knew better, but he didn't know I knew.

I had just finished eating when a tall, slim, long-legged man with black hair and sunglasses came strolling onto the terrace. "Good morning, all. Anybody miss me?" His smile was absolutely breathtaking.

For a moment the silence was deafening. Emily Kincade spoke first. "Oh, Michael, where have you been?" She asked it as though he were late coming home from the office. He'd been away for over two years.

He leaned down and kissed her cheek. "You're as beautiful as ever, Mother."

The greeting between Michael and his father was low-keyed and formal. Jason and Harvey gave Michael a less-than-enthusiastic greeting also. Amanda threw her napkin on the table. "You're an unpleasant surprise, Michael," she said as she rose from her chair.

Michael laughed. "Still mad because I exposed that boyfriend of yours when I was here last, little sister?" He laughed again.

J.B. spoke up. "Okay, Michael, don't start anything. You just arrived."

Amanda left the table with Ralph Satterly running along behind her. The exchange of greetings between Michael and Kyle bordered on friendly, and Gramps greeted his roving grandson with great affection. "Good to have you back, son," Gramps said. His eyes glistened. "You going to set Kincade Industries straight again?"

Michael laid his hand on Gramps's shoulder. "Only if it needs it, Gramps." He looked across the table at me. "And who do we have here? A new addition to the family?" He took off his sunglasses and gave me a wink with one of his big, gorgeous eyes.

The skin on my arms turned to gooseflesh. I smiled politely and a little uneasily while J.B. gave him a brief explanation for my presence at the ranch. Michael nodded and flashed a dazzling smile at me. "Very happy to meet you, Laura Grant. We'll have to get acquainted in the next few days. I'll look forward to it."

After a tearful greeting by both Mrs. Kiley and Marie Trent, Michael was served a king-size breakfast which he attacked with gusto. Michael was every bit as handsome as Jason, if not more so. His blue eyes danced continuously, his skin was tanned to a dark honey color, and energy and enthusiasm oozed from every pore. The man intrigued me, enchanted me, hypnotized me. The fact that he rarely took his eyes from me rattled me to my very core.

During that day I received all kinds of advice about

Michael. "Ignore him and don't trust him. We know nothing about him," Jason told me as we walked to the stable.

"Watch out for Michael. You never know what's going on in that flaky mind of his." That piece of advice came from Amanda, who hadn't spoken to me in three days.

Kyle didn't exactly warn me, but he was amused by Michael's arrival. "Jason had better watch out," he said. "Michael's loaded with charisma. You'd better watch out too, Laura."

"I can take care of myself, thank you, Kyle," I said curtly. He laughed quite loudly. I clamped my teeth and walked away from him.

J.B. frowned down at me just before dinner. "Laura, I'd like to tell you something. Michael is a charming fellow, but he lives by his wits somehow. A man like that usually has little value. It hurts me to say that about my own son, but you know I say what I think."

Indeed.

Mrs. Kiley said Michael was a love. Marie Trent called him a doll, and Gramps said he was the pick of the litter. This man, who received such mixed reviews, was the one who grabbed my arm and said I was going to be his dinner partner. His conversation at the dinner table was interesting and entertaining as he spoke about Saudi Arabia and South Africa and the Greek Islands, but he expertly skirted any and all questions as to what he might have been doing in such places. I went to bed wondering, like everyone else, I'm sure, just what Michael had been doing in such exotic locales.

My bedside clock said three-ten when the explosion occurred.

CHAPTER TWO

I LAY dead still for just a moment before I turned on a lamp and sprang out of bed. After grabbing my robe and shoving my feet into slippers, I raced out of my room. Michael, wearing jeans and an unbuttoned shirt, was running toward me from the end of the long hall. "Hey, Laura, what was that?"

"I haven't the foggiest."

Lights came on all over the house as we ran down the stairs to the first floor. J.B. and Kyle were standing in the doorway of my office when we arrived. I looked past them and sucked in my breath. I was vaguely aware that Emily and Amanda came up beside me, followed by Mrs. Kiley. Everyone was asking everyone else what happened. I stared at the papers scattered all over my desk and the floor. One of the French doors stood ajar, and the door to the wall safe was open.

Always the best-dressed man, Jason arrived dressed in pajamas, robe, and slippers. Ralph Satterly was behind him. I looked up at J.B. "I'm going to take a quick look. I won't touch anything." I knew what concerned him.

He nodded. "You can tell better than anyone if anything is missing."

"Shall I call the police?" I asked.

"Later," J.B. snapped. "Everyone else stay back here."

I tiptoed over the papers on the floor and glanced at the French doors. None of the glass had been shattered in the explosion, but I could see a hole in a pane of glass near the lock. I looked back at J.B. "I think the safe was opened and emptied before the explosion."

"Why do you say that?"

I noticed everyone stopped talking. "There's powderlike dust on top of all these papers here on my desk that I know I put in the safe last evening." I frowned. "Did anyone hear the dogs?" They were standing outside the French doors, wagging their tails.

Everyone shook his or her head no. Emily spoke up. "Why, Daisy didn't even let a murmur out of her. I wonder if she's getting hard of hearing."

I took a deep breath. "Whoever was in here tonight must have been someone the dogs and Daisy knew." I glanced at Emily, with Daisy in her arms. She considered Daisy every bit as much a watchdog as the big hounds, despite Daisy's teacup size.

Michael put his hands on his hips, threw his head back and laughed out loud. "In that case, dear friends and relatives, it was probably one of us."

The silence of the group was thunderous after Michael's quip, and then everyone began talking at once. It was a little surprising to me that everyone appeared to be more curious than upset or excited. If this sort of thing happened at my family's home, chaos would reign for some time.

I took the file key from its hiding place and made my way back to J.B., who was standing by the file cabinet. I glanced over at the group by the door as I unlocked the drawer of the file cabinet. Only Michael was watching me, with a half smile. Why did I think he was getting a kick out of all this? Was he merely amused, or did he have something to do with it? Preposterous! The man had been out of the country for over two years. Why would he come home and break into the new safe in his father's house?

J.B. placed his hand on my shoulder. "Has the file been touched?"

I shook my head. "It doesn't look like it. With the secrecy that surrounds Hardcase, I was going to suggest we use still another name for the progress charts. I filed them under Watson & Company since they owned the original patent."

J.B.'s brows knitted together tightly. "I wouldn't have thought it would be necessary for more secrecy in my own home, but I guess we'd better be careful. The specs are safe, aren't they?"

I pulled them out for him to see. I had them filed under expenses. He nodded, looking relieved. He glanced at the members of his household behind us.

Emily came up with the sanest idea for the moment. "Mrs. Kiley, will you please be so kind as to make a pot of coffee and bring it into the library?" She looked around at everyone. "Let's go into the library and wait for the police. Someone must call them, I suppose."

I watched her lead the procession across the foyer and into the library. She appeared to be taking complete control of the situation. Of all people, it was curious that she was the one to do it.

J.B. watched the group for a moment. "We'll be along in a minute," he said.

I looked at the French doors and gasped. Two men were looking in at us. It was a minute before I recognized them as the two men who lived on the ranch. J.B. spoke to them briefly. They turned and left. J.B. led the way into his bedroom through the connecting door from my office. "Come with me," he said over his shoulder.

He closed the door from the foyer and from Kyle's room on the other side of his bedroom. "For tonight we'll put the specs under my mattress. Tomorrow we'll find a better place for them. I doubt there's anything more planned for tonight."

I placed the specs between the mattress and the box spring, not sure it was the greatest idea, but it was his. With J.B. on top, no one was going to get to them tonight, anyway. I looked up at him and smiled. "Shall we join the others?"

"Yes, yes, by all means. We don't want this to get out of hand."

He took my arm, and we walked slowly into the

foyer. J.B. wore the merest hint of a grin. I felt rather smug myself. We'd outsmarted someone. But who? It had to be that file they were after. Nothing else in that safe was very valuable or very secret. Emily's and Amanda's jewels were kept in a safe upstairs. Maybe someone didn't know that. I couldn't buy that. The safe in my office was new, small, and hidden quite well in the wall behind a painting of a fiery-looking Indian.

Kyle met us at the library door. "Now take it easy, J.B.," he said softly. He took J.B.'s arm and winked at me. Whatever else Kyle might be, he did seem to be concerned for J.B.

When we walked into the library, Michael was on the phone. "Are you talking to the sheriff?" J.B. snapped at him. Michael nodded. "Hang up."

We were all stunned by J.B.'s tone, but Michael grinned as he said, "Wrong number," and hung up.

J.B. glared at him. "What did you tell them?"

Michael walked over to a chair and slouched down into it, totally undaunted by his father's tone. "You heard me tell the guy it was a wrong number. Aren't we going to let the law in on the latest of the family's scandalous doings?"

J.B. walked to a dark-blue velvet wing chair and allowed Kyle to help him lower himself into it. He looked around at everyone in the room. "No, Michael, I don't think we will tell the sheriff," he said softly. "You're right, of course—it does seem it has to be someone in this house who's involved in this. I think we should wash our own dirty laundry.

There's no sense telling the sheriff and letting the press get ahold of it. They'd have a field day besides possibly ruining any chance of success for Hardcase. It's the most secret and valuable project Kincade Industries has ever undertaken."

Gramps arrived just after J.B. and me. After he heard what had happened, he laughed out loud for a minute. "Hot dog, we've got some skulduggery in the clan again! Good thing you got home when you did, Michael. You were the one who cleaned up that last fine mess Amanda nearly got us into. You were the only one who wasn't too close to the forest to see the trees." He laughed heartily again. Amanda glared at her grandfather.

J.B. didn't appreciate his father's humor one bit. Mrs. Kiley arrived with the coffee just in time to squelch what could have been one of many irrelevant family squabbles. Emily poured. Gone was the flighty, confused, vague woman who appeared to be unsure of just about everything. She was every bit as coolheaded as Michael and Gramps. Jason sat motionless, with a noncommittal expression I couldn't begin to understand.

Harvey, on the other hand, was totally unglued. He yelled at J.B., "I told you that none of that Hardcase material should be out here!" He wiped perspiration from his forehead although the room was barely warm.

"Harvey, shut up!" J.B. snapped.

Gramps grinned. "Yes, Harvey, that's always a good idea for you."

"Look, Father, I know—"

Gramps cut Harvey off. "Harvey, when are you going to learn you don't know one-tenth of what you think you know?" He scowled at J.B. "Anything missing?"

J.B. shook his head. His jaw was taut. His face appeared pink. His breathing was labored. "We know the Hardcase material isn't missing, and that's the most important thing we have in this house." He took a deep breath. "Laura can let us know in the morning if anything is missing. I doubt there is." He looked over at me. "Laura, you and I are the only ones with the combination to that safe. What did you do with your slip of paper that contained the combination?"

"I memorized the combination, and then I disposed of the slip of paper."

"How did you dispose of it?"

"I took it to the kitchen and, using an ashtray, I burned it."

"Did anyone see you do it? Is it possible you said what it was to anyone?"

I shook my head. "No, there was no one in the kitchen but Mrs. Kiley, and we didn't discuss what I was doing. We talked about the pork chops she was stuffing. When my paper had burned to ashes, I put water on it to be sure the fire was out and then put it in the trash."

Mrs. Kiley, who was in the process of refilling our coffee cups, spoke up. "That's right, J.B. I didn't know what she was burning, but I told her I was glad her compulsion for arson was so limited."

I had to ask. "J.B., what did you do with your slip containing the combination?" Since he had opened the safe only once, I guessed he'd held on to the slip of paper.

He grimaced. "This is my house, and the people who live here are either my family or people I trust without reservation. I didn't really think I had to worry about anyone under this roof." His voice rose in volume as he spoke. His face was getting redder by the moment.

Kyle squeezed his shoulders. "Take a deep breath, J.B.," he said softly.

J.B. took in a deep breath, held it for a moment, and let it out slowly. He lowered his voice. "I folded the paper and put it in the back of the middle drawer of the desk in my bedroom. Will you go and see if it's there, Laura?"

I leaped to my feet, glad to escape from that room. Tension charged the air. Michael followed me. He started talking as soon as we stepped into the foyer. "I've seen the old man shook many times, but I don't think I've ever seen him in the state he's in right now."

"Your father has reason to be shook. We think our intruder is after the biggest, most important, most secretive project Kincade Industries has ever undertaken. You wouldn't believe the steps we've taken to keep it secret or the enormity of what it involves. It could be worth many, many millions. Also—"

Michael interrupted me as he pushed open the door to J.B.'s room. "Also, since it looks like one of his family may be out to steal the formula or whatever, it's hard on his ego."

I stepped into J.B.'s room ahead of Michael. "Come on, that's not fair. Don't be so hard on your father. It wouldn't be easy for most people to accept the possibility that one of their own family would sabotage the family business."

"My, what loyalty! If only J.B. could get that kind of loyalty from his family. Alas, it can't be bred. It wouldn't surprise me to know someone in this family is sabotaging, or helping to sabotage, Kincade Industries. It wouldn't be the first time. There has been a lot of family shenanigans connected with that firm during the three generations it's been operating. It's one of the reasons I want no part of being one of the fourth generation to run it. Jason will enjoy that. Tell me, pretty lady, what is Hardcase?"

I looked up at him and saw the teasing glint in his eyes. I went to the desk. "My lips are sealed. It's secret, remember?"

He laughed. I found the piece of paper with the combination of the safe neatly typed on it. It was folded into a small wad. I closed the desk drawer. Michael was rubbing the lead of a pencil over a third notepad. "Aha!" he said rather dramatically.

"Aha, what?" I asked, looking over his shoulder.

"Grammar-school stuff maybe, but here's where someone copied the combination down, I'd bet." He shoved the pad over to me. "Is this it?"

It was and it gave me my first real suspect. Kyle spent a lot of time in J.B.'s room. We took the pad into the library and handed it to J.B. with the small wad of paper from his desk drawer. He clucked his tongue and looked around at the group. "It hurts me deeply to know that one of you is a traitor to our family and our ancestors." His voice turned from sorrowful to angry in a split second. "Believe me, when I find out who is behind this, they will pay much more dearly than they ever dreamed."

I think we all flinched a little. Only Kyle smiled thinly and laid his hand on J.B.'s shoulder again to settle him down.

Gramps spoke up with a twinkle in his eye. "Every generation has a simpleton and a rotter, J.B. We know the simpleton is our pretty little Amanda, who was duped by the handsome engineer who had ambitious plans and larceny in his heart. If it hadn't been for Michael, he might have gotten away with it too."

"Gramps, stop it!" Amanda had been uncustomarily quiet, but now her voice had a razor-sharp edge to it. "Maybe it's Michael this time. It's interesting that he arrived in that expensive white sports car just this morning. Don't forget, everyone, we have no idea how my big brother makes his living."

Michael laughed. "I have no idea what Hardcase is and, frankly, I don't care."

"That's what you say." She spat the words at him.

Whatever had gone on between them a couple of years ago must have been monumental for such hard feelings still to be lingering. My curiosity was peaked.

Michael shrugged and brought up something I'd forgotten about. "Doesn't this house have a security system anymore? It used to have an alarm that sounded like a parade of fire engines if anything outside activated it after midnight."

Silence fell on the room for a moment. Then J.B. answered him. "Yes, we still have that alarm. It's on an automatic timer now. It comes on at midnight and goes off at seven in the morning. Everyone in the house has a key to shut it off if they go in or out during those hours." He looked at each one of us individually. I had a key, but I'd never used it since I'd never been outside the house between midnight and seven in the morning.

Michael raised his eyebrows and looked at his hands. Everyone was quiet until Gramps broke the silence. He looked over at Ralph Satterly, who for once wasn't smiling. He was sitting on the arm of Amanda's chair, with his hand on her shoulder, and looking as though he'd like to be somewhere else.

"You, young man," Gramps said quite sharply.

Ralph's body jerked. "Yes, sir?"

"How much do you know about Hardcase?"

"Nothing, sir. I work in the accounting department. We never know what goes on in the labs."

Next Gramps looked at his son Harvey. "Harvey, are you sure, with your big mouth and ego, that you didn't tell someone outside of the company that you pulled quite a coup by getting Watson & Company to bring the Hardcase project to us for research and development?"

Harvey, a man in his fifties, for a moment looked like a small boy about to explain a lousy report card.

"Father, of course not. I don't discuss company business with outsiders."

Gramps laughed. "I've always prayed not." He looked around the room at the rest of us and then up at Marie Trent, who was leaning on the back of his wheelchair. "Well, Rambo, we've got quite a mystery here. We know that J.B., Harvey, Laura, and young Jason, who's been very quiet tonight, know about the Hardcase project. It would seem, if they have larceny in their hearts, they could get what they wanted without waking up the whole blamed household. Now, the bookkeeper here doesn't know anything, he says, but bookkeepers rarely do. Michael just arrived, so it's not likely he'd know anything about it. We never know what Kyle knows, do we?"

Kyle gave him a playful grin. "Now, Gramps. Oh, that I could be as sly as you."

Gramps laughed. "That leaves the ladies. Emily stays so busy, she probably wouldn't have time for industrial espionage. Of course, no one really knows just what she stays busy at, do we?"

Emily closed her eyes for a moment. "Now, Father, I'm hardly in a position to care about espionage, industrial or otherwise." She laughed. "I'm surprised that Kincade Industries does such cloak-and-dagger stuff."

Gramps narrowed his eyes. I wondered if he believed her. I also wondered why he wouldn't. He turned his attention to his granddaughter. "Now, I doubt Amanda is the least concerned with what goes on at Kincade Industries as long as there's money for her to buy clothes and change her hair color and have parties at the drop of a hat. I rather think she learned her lesson a couple of years ago. At least, I hope so."

Amanda jumped to her feet. "Gramps. . . ." She stalked toward the door. "I'm going to bed." She left the room.

I stared after her. She had asked me if I was working on Hardcase! Why didn't she mention that she knew about it and where she'd heard about it? The more I got to know her, the harder it was to believe J.B. might have told her about Hardcase. They argued a lot, and he rarely seemed to approve of anything she did. It seemed at times she disagreed with him just for the sake of disagreement. I'd even broken up their arguments a few times because of J.B.'s health. Why on earth would he explain a secret project to her when they seldom spoke a civil word to each other? But where else would she have heard about it?

J.B. hit the arm of his chair with his palm. "All right, Dad, that's enough for tonight." He looked at Jason. "You and Harvey see what you can do to cover up that hole in the French door in Laura's office. It's supposed to rain by morning. The rest of us had better get some rest. We'll try to sort this out in the morning." Kyle helped him to stand and, together, they left the library. Everyone else filed out after them.

I stood and found Michael beside me. "This may be an interesting few days, after all," he said gleefully.

I agreed wholeheartedly, but I only nodded. We

were the last to leave the library, and I noticed that he wore his watch. "Do you always wear your watch to bed?"

"Always."

I picked up his wrist and looked at it. It was a very sophisticated model and did a lot of things I didn't even care about. I looked at the sunburst clock on the wall. "I'd say your watch is running about fifteen minutes fast these days." I nodded to the clock as I spoke.

He grinned down at me. "I checked that clock when I went to bed. It agreed with my watch. Look back at the grandfather clock in the library. It agrees with my watch but for a couple of minutes."

I frowned up at him. "We must have lost our electricity for fifteen minutes."

Michael chuckled as he took my arm and aimed me toward the stairs. "You're a smart one, you are."

"It could mean the area lost power," I said. "We can check on that in the morning. Of course, someone may have shut off our power for fifteen minutes." I looked up at him and grinned. The intrigue of all this was stimulating. I'd never been even remotely involved in any kind of intrigue.

Michael's eyes danced as he looked down at me. "Right. Maybe someone shut off the electricity long enough to get in, do their dastardly deed, and get out. On their way out they turned the electricity back on. If it was someone in the family, the dogs probably helped."

I frowned again as we reached the top of the stairs.

"If it wasn't family or someone from this house, where were the dogs? How would someone else know where the fuse boxes were? How did they get through the gate?

Michael fought a grin. "You'd make a good detective. Here's something else to think about. People rarely verify the time when they're awakened suddenly at three in the morning. It's Sunday. It's not likely any of us has appointments. If it wasn't noticed until, say, late morning, who'd be able to pinpoint when the electricity had gone off? With the stove and refrigerator and freezer and hot-water heater on butane, Mrs. Kiley wouldn't notice it during the morning as long as she didn't need the lights on."

Interesting.

While I lay in bed, waiting for sleep, I thought of Michael Kincade, with his shiny black hair and his dancing eyes. He was the type of man who made me feel better just being around him. I grimaced at the dark ceiling as I thought of all the bad press I heard about him from his family. Well, he wouldn't be around long, Mrs. Kiley said, and he might be fun to know for a while.

It was a shame Jason didn't have more of Michael's . . . what? Charisma, Kyle had called it. The man sparkled. Yes, that's what it was. Michael sparkled. I laughed at myself as I turned over. Besides myself, Michael was probably the only person I could be absolutely certain had nothing to do with the break-in. After all, he had no involvement with Kincade Industries. Secure with that thought, I drifted off to sleep.

CHAPTER THREE

IT was nine o'clock when I woke from a bad dream. I thought I'd seen the lab that was working on Hardcase blow sky high. Hardcase was a paint. But hardly an ordinary paint. Watson & Company had purchased the patent for a paint that was scratch-proof and chipproof. Kincade Industries was doing some research and development on that paint in an effort to make it applicable to automobiles. From what I understood, it was a given that every large automaker in the world was ready to stand in line with a blank check for whoever could supply this paint. Watson & Company and Kincade Industries, one of the pioneers in research and development, wanted their names to be inserted on that blank check. Apparently somebody, somewhere had other ideas.

I showered, dressed, and went downstairs. I glanced at the sunburst clock in the foyer. It said nine forty-five. My watch said ten. I idly wondered where Michael might be.

Because I wasn't a big breakfast eater, Mrs. Kiley usually placed a thermos of coffee and two muffins on my desk each morning. It was a surprise to see Jason sitting behind my desk, going through papers, drinking my coffee, and eating one of my muffins. I hesitated a minute before I entered. "Good morning, Jason. Find anything interesting?" I poured myself a cup of coffee and tried to pretend I wasn't annoyed.

"Good morning, Laura. I'm trying to organize this mess that was taken from the safe last night. I know you moved the copy of the specifications for the Hardcase project. Would you mind getting it for me? We must find a safe place for it. That was close last night."

I glared at him. Jason's name was *not* on the confidential list of names of the people who were authorized to see the specs. He knew this. Why was he asking to see them? "Jason, you know I can't give you those specs. Your name isn't on the authorization list."

He let out a long, bored sigh. "You have a reputation for being a stickler for details. It's said that nothing gets by you. I guess that's one of the many reasons we consider you such a valuable employee." He smiled. "It's merely an oversight that my name wasn't placed on that list. I'll talk to Father when he wakes."

He looked back at the papers in front of him. "By the way, Uncle Harvey and I have decided to close this office. We knew it was a bad idea from the beginning. It's too dangerous for you and Father to have the Hardcase information here. We'll inform Father this afternoon." He looked up at me. "I'll help you pack up the paperwork. We'll send the trucks out to pick up the equipment and boxes in the morning."

I stared at Jason for a moment. He smiled thinly before he returned his attention to the papers in front of him. Nothing sounded right. Jason and Harvey didn't make decisions and then *inform* J.B. There was no sign that either J.B. or I was in danger. And I knew for a fact that it was determined neither Jason nor Harvey would need access to the specs. I was there when the decision was made. Those of us who were authorized had to sign in four different places on four different days so that normal differences in our signatures would be on record and, therefore, verifiable when we needed a set of specs.

And J.B. would *not* bend the rules and allow unauthorized use of those specs for Jason or anyone. Even Jason's tone of voice didn't sound right. His smile didn't seem quite right. It was as though I were a new employee he'd just met. I felt like telling him he *did* know me. I clenched my fists. *What's going on here?* I asked myself, beginning to seethe.

"Jason, do you want to tell me what's going on? You're not acting like yourself, and you're acting as though we just met yesterday. Are you testing me by asking to see those specs?" I wasn't the calm, cool, and collected Laura Grant he'd known for so long. I was a mad Laura Grant. I knew it showed, and I didn't care.

He smiled. "Now, Laura, you know better than that. I have a lot of pressure on me right now." His voice was even, but he glanced up at me with his eyes opened wide. "Laura, you seem upset."

"I *am* upset," I answered sharply.

He frowned for a moment but spoke again in his normal voice. "I'm surprised. I thought you were one of those few admirable women who had full control of their emotions. I don't think I've ever heard you sound angry before."

"Well, you're hearing me now. If you're testing me, I want to know it. I've never known you to be absentminded; therefore, you know I can't give you those specs. If you think I'll do it just because"—I hesitated, looking for a way to say it—"we've gotten to know each other better this past month, with all our picnics and horseback riding, you're sadly mistaken and I'm insulted." I didn't sound a bit friendly. The more I thought of it, the angrier I got.

He cleared his throat and looked at the French doors. If I hadn't been so riled, I might have laughed. Was he looking for an escape route? Right then I recognized a chip in the armor of Kincade Industries' Prince Charming. Contrary to popular belief, Jason's adverse reaction to women who showed emotion wasn't because he felt they were unstable, but because they frightened him. The more I glared at him, the more nervous he became and the more my anger ebbed. I finally had to fight a grin.

He cleared his throat several times before he finally looked back at me. "I'm sorry if I've upset you, Laura." He cleared his throat again and went on reluctantly, "Uncle Harvey wants everything back at the office tomorrow, and he's acting as though it's my fault that this office was set up in the first place. We'll take care of everything as soon as Dad is available." He looked back at the papers again.

I felt dismissed. My anger returned. I glanced toward the door and noticed Michael leaning against the doorjamb, wearing that half smile of his.

"Who says the decision about closing this office is yours and Uncle Harvey's to make, little brother?" he asked. "The chairman of the board and the president of this privately held corporation may have something to say about it."

Jason glared at Michael. "As I see it, big brother, it's none of your business."

"Oh, you've got that right, but I've always enjoyed the games the people in this family play. I suspect that Father will pull rank on you and Uncle Harvey. After all, he is the president of said corporation as well as its chief executive officer." He turned to me. "That's still the way it is, isn't it, Laura?"

"Yes," I answered, none too happy to be involved in this conversation.

Michael was obviously enjoying himself. "So I thought," he said. "Also, Gramps loves having this operation here. He says he even loves Laura Grant. Did you know that, little brother?"

"Gramps is old and—"

"Ah, but he's still chairman of the board. I wouldn't write him off so quickly, Jason. Some people get old, while some just have a lot of birthdays. Don't underestimate Gramps." Michael raised his coffee mug in my direction and nodded slightly. "And how is the beautiful Laura Grant this morning?"

Out of the corner of my eye I caught Jason's deep frown. I'm quite sure I wasn't supposed to fraternize with the enemy. However, I wasn't ready to choose up sides in this family. Not yet, anyway. "I'm fine, thank you." I wished I knew Michael better. I wished I knew how much of his bad press was deserved. Being almost as much of an outsider as I, yet knowing everyone involved so well, he might be able to understand some things that bothered me.

What it amounted to was I needed someone to talk to. Why hadn't Amanda admitted that she knew about the Hardcase project? Why did Jason ask for the specs when he knew he wasn't authorized? Surely he didn't think I'd just give them to him. Why was he acting so strange this morning? Why was he going through the papers from the safe? What else had he and Harvey talked about after everyone went to bed? What was the real reason he wanted to close the office there at the ranch? I felt there was more to it than he mentioned. Was Jason involved in that safe explosion? Hardly. What about Kyle? What about Amanda?

Amanda did bother me, but I wasn't sure why. She was hardly a brain. In fact, I often wondered if she had one at all under all that bleached, crimped hair. Was she involved with someone other than Ralph who may be interested in Hardcase? Again, not likely, but . . . Ralph didn't seem her type. I couldn't fathom that Ralph would have anything to do with this. The man had nerves of pure jelly. Was she using Ralph for a cover while she was really involved with someone else?

The buzzer on my desk interrupted my thoughts. I realized both Jason and Michael were watching me. I hit the button and said good morning to J.B.

"Come in here a minute, Laura," he said briskly.

Kyle gave me a bright greeting when I walked into the room. J.B. sat in a big chair, dressed in pajamas, a blue satin robe, and slippers, watching Kyle smooth the sheets on his bed. J.B. held a large manila envelope in his hand. The clock on his bedside table was fifteen minutes slow. Before I could mention the electricity lapse, J.B. started talking to Kyle about his breakfast. "Tell Mrs. Kiley I'll take it in here this morning." He waved the envelope in the air as he spoke.

J.B. was being very open and obvious with that envelope, I thought. I knew it was the one I'd given him the night before with the specs inside. There was a cross on it made with a red marking pen. I had done that to scratch out a note on the envelope. Was the show of the envelope on purpose and he was testing Kyle? Why? J.B. usually had a reason for everything he did or said.

Kyle nodded and pulled a comforter up over the king-sized bed. J.B. handed me the envelope. "You take care of this, Laura." His voice seemed louder than usual. Were his eyes trying to tell me something?

I took the envelope and frowned. "Of course, J.B."

I wasn't about to ask questions with Kyle in the room.

I walked up the stairs with as much nonchalance as I could manage. My knees were shaking, mostly because of the responsibility I carried in my right hand, but partly because I knew Michael and Jason were watching me from my office doorway. I could hardly hide the big, bulky manila envelope since I was wearing a white silk long-sleeved blouse and a straight pink skirt. Did Jason realize I had the specs in that envelope? Of course.

I went to my room and looked around. It was a sitting-room-and-bedroom combination, well furnished in a contemporary style and decorated in white and many shades of blue. It was a comfortable setting, and I had been very comfortable in it, until that day. The pictures on the walls were scenes of wooded areas with waterfalls and ponds. An abundance of tall pine trees and cedar trees were framed by the large windows. It all spelled serenity. At that moment, however, I didn't have a serene spot in my whole body.

There were normal places to hide an envelope, such as under the mattress, under my underwear, or rolled up in one of my boots, but every TV watcher knew those places. I felt nervous and imagined someone was watching me. It was ridiculous, but that morning I felt everything and everyone at the ranch was a bit ridiculous. Why had J.B. given this to me, I wondered. Was I the only one in the house he trusted? Maybe. How sad.

Suddenly I felt inspired. I changed into a pair of brown tweed pants and a bulky beige sweater. I tucked the envelope into the waist of my pants and, if a bit uncomfortable, it was nicely concealed under my sweater.

I took the back stairs down to the kitchen and hoped Mrs. Kiley was close to being ready to deliver J.B.'s breakfast. I also hoped she wouldn't ask too many questions. Luckily she was setting up his tray. Her eyebrows shot up when I stepped through the narrow back door. "You're a surprise. Hardly anyone has used those stairs since the kids grew up. How are you this morning?"

"Fine, Mrs. Kiley. And you?"

"Tired, if you want to know. His nibs, Jason, was banging around in here looking for something to eat way before seven this morning. After last night I thought everyone would sleep late, and I planned on a little of it myself. Anybody know yet who got us all up in the middle of the night?"

I shook my head while I took a mug from the cupboard. "Not that I've heard." I filled the mug with coffee and made a face. "I may hide out in here today."

She picked up the tray. "Be glad to have your company. Got to take J.B. his breakfast. I'll be right back."

When she went out the door, I grabbed the short stepladder she kept by the refrigerator and climbed up on the second step. From there I could reach the cupboard above the refrigerator. Mrs. Kiley had shown me a stack of old cookbooks she'd had for over thirty years that she didn't use anymore. "With new appliances and new mixes and new food combinations, they're as out of style as the clothes of those times," she had said.

I placed the big thick envelope under the cookbooks, closed the cupboard door, and put the ladder away quickly. It wasn't a great place to hide the envelope, but it wasn't a place anyone was liable to look for it or stumble across it accidentally. I was anxious to tell J.B. where I'd put it.

I passed Mrs. Kiley in the foyer. "I've thought of a few things I have to do," I told her.

When I walked into my office, Jason was standing in the open doorway to his father's room. J.B. was talking. "Don't worry about the specs, Jason. Laura has taken care of them. I'll meet with you and Harvey in the library as soon as I finish my breakfast." He looked up at the door from the foyer. "Amanda, has your mood improved since we saw you last?"

"I just stopped by to see if you knew who blew the safe yet." Her voice sounded bored.

"No, and I'd appreciate it if you didn't broadcast the matter among your friends," J.B. said gruffly.

She shrugged. "Ralph and I are going to play tennis. The rain has stopped." She hesitated a moment before she went on, "I hope everyone remembers I'm having a few people in tonight to welcome Tina home from Europe. We're using the guest house."

J.B. grimaced. "Who'd dare interfere with a party you've planned?"

Jason turned around and was surprised to see me. He closed the door. "Thanks for not mentioning anything about closing this office to my father. We'll take care of it. Father says you've taken care of the specs for Hardcase." He picked up my hands. "I'm sorry I was so offish this morning. Uncle Harvey is really shook. You know how he can get. I didn't mean to take it out on you." He squeezed my hands and gave me that smile that lit up the world. He seemed more like himself.

I squeezed his hands back. "We'll forget it, Jason." I never could stay mad for very long at a time. "I think I'll take a walk. The air always smells nice after a rain."

"I'd go with you, but I'm waiting for Father."

I stepped out through the French doors and patted the two dogs. I invited them to walk along with me while I sorted out my thoughts. I was sorry Jason wanted to close the office at the ranch. I loved it here, for one thing. My life in the city was not so exciting that I was eager to return. In fact, it had been rather ho-hum for quite a while. And, though not an insurmountable problem, I didn't have a place to live!

Because the break-in appeared to be an inside job, was everyone going to ignore it? I couldn't believe that. J.B. couldn't tolerate an unsolved riddle any more than I could.

I looked off ahead of me and smiled at the tall trees weaving gently in the slight breeze. It was very doubtful I'd have to be concerned about going back to the city very soon. J.B. and Gramps liked the information I was able to obtain for them at any given time. Neither of them would be willing to give it up. And they had the power to keep everything status quo.

I saw Michael coming toward me. The dogs raced ahead to greet him. My father used to say that you can trust a man when dogs and cats like him, but watch out for him if they don't. Well, the dogs certainly loved Michael. They had nearly gone crazy when they first saw him after he arrived, and they were certainly happy now.

I wondered if Michael had anything to do with the fact that I didn't want to leave the ranch. Of course not. What a silly thought! I'd just met him the day before amid the worst publicity of any other single person I'd ever met.

His smile was playful as he approached me. "Escaping?" he asked.

"Just strolling," I said and smiled without intending to.

"You might like to know—I called the power company this morning, and I guess we were the only ones in the area that had a break in our service. Also, I checked around the two power panels and found absolutely nothing. The rain, after our break-in, would have washed out any tracks that might have been there."

"Michael, even if someone they knew was prowling around, wouldn't the dogs be a little disturbed until they saw who it was?"

He was thoughtful for a minute. "At night they

might let out a bark or two, but as soon as they saw a friend, they'd stop."

"Wouldn't someone inside hear the bark?"

"Probably, but if one is half asleep, one rarely pays much attention to two or three barks from dogs. Especially if they quit suddenly. It could be a cat or a deer or the moon. Dogs spook easily at night."

He had a point. I started walking, and Michael fell in beside me. He picked up my hand. "I noticed my little brother holding your hand on the way to the stable yesterday. How serious is it between you two?"

I pulled my hand back. "It's not serious at all. Jason and I ride together sometimes. He was my boss for a while." I wondered if I was talking too fast.

Michael smiled mischievously. "Good. I like to ride too. Now, tell me about Laura Grant."

I stopped at the fence of the corral and watched the horses frolicking across the paddock. "They are so beautiful." I knew he was watching me. "There's not much to tell about Laura Grant. I do think hearing about Michael Kincade would be a lot more interesting. It sounds as though you've been everywhere. How do you happen to be such a world traveler?"

"I go for opportunities, for work, for fun," he said as he looked off at the horizon. "I like to see different parts of the world and different cultures."

"Sounds exciting. What kind of work or opportunities take you to places like the Greek Islands and South Africa?"

"Now you sound like the family." He grinned down at me. "You know, traveling loses its charm after a while. About six months ago I decided it was time I stayed home. I've even thought of settling down." He leaned against the fence. "By staying home I mean staying in the States, not here at the ranch."

"Would you consider working for Kincade Industries?"

"Not for a minute."

"What would you do?"

"I'd find something to keep me out of trouble." He was being evasive, as he had been at dinner the night before, but his eyes twinkled mischievously.

It was so childish of him to keep his life such a secret, unless. . . . I'd pursue that thought later. "From what I hear, no one has ever known what you do for a living. I think it worries your parents." In reality, I thought it just annoyed his family that they didn't know. I was just plain curious.

"As long as I don't bring bad press to the family name and don't ask for money, my father is willing to tolerate my nomadic life, as he calls it. He expects me to come, with my hat or my debts or my pride in my hand someday, and ask for a job at Kincade Industries. It riles him that I haven't. Now tell me about you."

I looked up at the darkening sky. "It may rain again soon."

"Now who's evading the subject?"

I looked up at him. "I'm not evading anything." I felt a little testy. "You're a great one to talk. You keep your life locked up in secrecy."

"Do you play that game too?"

He was laughing at me. "I have nothing to hide," I said sarcastically. "I grew up in L.A. in a very normal family. I have an older brother and sister. I went to State College and graduated with a degree in computer games, according to my father. I lasted six months at a company that designs computer programs for huge corporations. I didn't like it much. Kincade Industries offered me a good job with a lot of potential, so I moved to Sacramento and took it. Three years later, here I am."

"I think there's more, but I'll let it go for now." He peered at my face and picked up my hand and squeezed it. "Do you know you're not only beautiful, but you have the most beautiful blue eyes I've ever seen? I'm sure you know the strong affect they can have on a man."

I jerked my hand away from him. "That line may go over in the Greek Islands from an American playboy in a cocktail lounge at night, but here on a ranch, standing beside the horse corral on a cloudy morning, it bombs." My words had come out crisply. I turned and marched away from the fence and headed back toward the house.

From the corner of my eye I saw him throw back his head and laugh. That arrogant, self-centered, conceited excuse for a man probably thought I'd swoon at his stale line! How dare he think I'd be susceptible to that sort of sophomoric, outdated flattery?

He caught up with me and placed his hand on my arm. "Hey, wait a minute. Let me apologize." He was still smiling. "I'm sorry. I don't think that came out the way I intended. Can we start over again? Please?"

I glanced up at him. His expression looked boyish and sincere, but his eyes were still dancing. I kept walking but slowed my pace. We were walking uphill, and I was becoming breathless. He stayed with me, watching me, waiting for my answer. "Look, there's no reason for us to start over," I said. "You don't have to apologize. Let's just forget it."

"I don't want to forget it. I want to start over with you. How do you do?" he said formally. "I'm Michael Kincade."

I glanced at him again and, against my will, smiled at both his pseudo-serious expression and his outstretched hand as he walked beside me. I fought it, but finally I stopped and took his hand in mine and shook it. "How do you do, Michael Kincade? I'm Laura Grant." We tried to keep straight faces, but we broke out into laughter at the same moment.

He placed his arm around my shoulders. "Laura Grant, you have no idea how glad I am to know you."

Mrs. Kiley broke the spell. She called to us from a second-story window. "Laura, Michael, come up here. Hurry!" There was urgency in her voice.

CHAPTER FOUR

MICHAEL and I raced into the house, across the foyer and up the stairs. The usually unflappable Mrs. Kiley was breathless when we reached her. "Laura, you just won't believe it."

"What is it, Mrs. Kiley?" I laid my hand on her arm.

"J.B. sent me to find you. I got to your door and found. . . ." She took my hand and pulled me. "Come see for yourself."

At my bedroom door I stopped in my tracks. A page from my large desk calendar was taped to the door. The writing was childish but very clear. *Laura Grant,* was scrawled in big black letters across the top. The rest was written with a red marking pen. *We know you have the specs. Don't leave this ranch until we have them, or someone in this family will pay dearly. We'll let you know how you can help.*

I drew in my breath. "What on earth. . . ."

Michael read it twice before he spoke. He took one of my hands in his and squeezed it tightly. He pushed open the door, and my mouth dropped open. The mattress was lying on the floor, the cushions to the couch and chair had been carelessly thrown around, and two chairs lay on their sides. All the lamps were lying on the floor, and the contents of the dresser drawers were spread around the room. The closet door was open, and all my clothes had been pulled out and thrown on the couch.

"You go in and see if anything is missing. I doubt J.B. will want to call the sheriff about this, either," Mrs. Kiley said with a touch of annoyance.

"I can't think of anything I have here that anyone would want," I said. I stepped into the room, more angry than anything else. Surely, whoever was looking for the Hardcase specs wouldn't bother with my wallet or the few dollars it contained. I was right. The few pieces of gold jewelry I had in a small jewelry box were in place also. Who'd think I'd be so dumb as to hide those specs in my room? I picked up two cushions from the floor. "I don't think anything's missing. We know what they were looking for, of course, but they didn't find it."

Mrs. Kiley set her jaw. "What they did do is make a mighty fine mess. I'm going to get Kyle to help straighten it up." She went to the top of the stairs and yelled down to Kyle in the library.

"What do you want?" he yelled back.

"Come up here and help us put Laura's room back together. Somebody's ransacked it. It's a bloody mess."

Jason stepped out of his room three doors away from mine. "What's all the racket?" He looked as though he might have been napping. Or he hoped someone thought he was napping. Why did that thought enter my mind? Ralph Satterly stepped out of his room across the hall but didn't say a word.

"Somebody's ransacked Laura's room," Michael said. "He left this for her." He handed the note to Jason.

Jason read the note and came to my side. He slipped his arm around my waist and pulled me to him. "Oh, no!" he said softly.

Kyle bounded up the stairs and let out a low whistle when he saw the condition of the room. Jason turned me around. "We'll straighten up in there. You can wait in my room." He looked over at Ralph. "Where's Amanda?"

"She's down in the kitchen fixing some hot chocolate. I'll get her." He took off toward the stairs like a scared rabbit.

"Look, Jason, if you guys will just put the mattress back and pick up the furniture, I'll put my things away," I said. "I'm all right, really." I smiled weakly. My anger was turning into rage, and it was barely below the surface. How dare anyone go through my personal things?

Amanda showed up, breathless. She, too, gasped at the sight. Michael and Jason followed Kyle into the room, each of them carefully picking his way, stepping over cushions and bedding and lamps.

"I guess the same goes for this mess as I said about the safe this morning," Michael said. "It has to be one of us. Isn't that a splendid thought? I wonder what's next on the agenda." He did *not* have to look so amused! Jason frowned, but Kyle raised his eyebrows and looked as though he, too, were amused by the thought.

J.B. called from the bottom of the stairs. Mrs. Kiley went to the banister and told him what was going on. He mumbled something I couldn't hear and then asked, "Does anyone have any idea where my wife might be?"

No one did. No one, in fact, had seen her since we all left the library about four-thirty that morning.

Again this family amazed me. No one appeared to be overly alarmed about Emily Kincade's absence, only curious. In my family, my mother's unaccounted-for absence for a whole morning would cause full-scale hysteria.

While the men straightened the furniture, I made my way over to the windows and looked down on the rolling lawn. Whoever had ransacked my room could have kept a good eye on me while we were at the corral and making our short trip back to the house. That would let Michael out, since he was with me. I bit my lip. Of course, he could have gone to my room right after I changed my clothes and left for the kitchen. I didn't see him from the time I took the envelope to my room until I met him down near the corral.

Except for J.B. and Gramps, who couldn't climb stairs, Michael was probably the one with the least reason to tear my room apart for those specs. Jason and Kyle and probably Amanda, Ralph, and Uncle Harvey knew J.B. gave me that envelope.

With the furniture and lamps back in order and the bed made, I assured everyone I would rather put my things away myself. Everyone left but Michael. "I'll wait so you can join me in a hot chocolate when you finish." He glanced at Jason and flashed him a big smile as Jason stepped out into the hall. Michael looked over at me and shrugged. "I don't think I made his day."

"I don't think you ever make his day."

He grinned. "I never try." He sat down on the arm of a big chair as I, a bit self-consciously, folded my lingerie and placed it in a drawer. He watched me more closely than I liked. "Laura, be honest with me—do you have any idea who in this illustrious family might be after those specs?"

"Not a clue," I answered honestly. "A few things bother me, but I'm not sure if they mean much."

"I don't suppose you'd share them with me."

I wanted to tell him about the things that were bugging me, but I hesitated. "I don't have them sorted out that well yet. Maybe later, when I know for sure what's bothering me."

"That's a nice diversionary tactic until you make up your mind about me."

I shot him a sharp look. I wasn't too thrilled that he could read me that well.

He went on without waiting for a comment from me. "I know there's security attached to most research and development, but is there as much security around everything at Kincade Industries these days as there is around this Hardcase project?"

I thought for a minute. "Yes and no. There's more security on some things than there is on others, of course. As far as I know, there's never been quite the security on anything as there is on Hardcase, but, then again, I guess there's never been anything that has the potential of being quite as valuable, either."

He folded one of my sweaters, quite neatly, and handed it to me. "Do you know the real reason Jason and Uncle Harvey want to close up this office? I don't buy that it's safety for you and my father."

I shook my head. "No, I don't." I wondered why Michael wondered about it.

He hesitated for a minute, and then he said thoughtfully, "It could be that Harvey is worried about what decisions my father and Gramps might make without his knowing about them. I'm sure he's a regular busybody at the office, just as he's always been everywhere else. Maybe he and Jason are afraid of losing control, whatever that might mean."

"It wouldn't mean much. Your father rules pretty much with an iron hand. It's true that he can issue instructions via the computer that neither Harvey nor Jason might find out about until later, whereas at the office he might have one of them hand out the instructions. And Harvey does like to think he's in on everything that goes on, even though most of us know better." I grinned sheepishly. I hated talking about his relatives like that, but he was the one to bring it up. "I don't know. I doubt that's the whole reason."

He stood up. "Look, I don't want to disillusion you about Jason if there's something brewing between you two, but—"

I interrupted him. "There is nothing between us," I snapped. "Do go on."

"Okay, okay, don't get huffy. You should know that although Jason may have a lot of the good traits I missed, he has rarely done anything that wasn't to help himself. Amanda used to say he raised self-serving to a science. Not that she doesn't do the same thing and maybe more. Anyway, I'd like to know the real reason they're hot to close up this office. I have a feeling it could be important. Gramps says he and Father have been able to expedite a great many things with you and your equipment here. For one thing, they're spared the constant interruptions they have to endure at the office. Gramps would have set up this arrangement long ago if he'd realized how well it would work."

I raised my eyebrows. "They both like the instantaneous control this setup allows them." I finished putting things in the dresser drawers and moved over to the closet.

Michael handed me a jacket. "Do either Amanda or Kyle have anything to do with the business these days?" I shook my head. "Very interesting," he said with a grin. "Soon after you went upstairs this morning, Kyle went up. I went up a few minutes later and found him and Amanda talking in hushed tones near her door. I heard Kyle say, 'He gave it to Laura to take care of.' " He picked up another jacket and looked around for a hanger.

I took the jacket from him. "I guess everyone knew that envelope contained the specs. What else? J.B. was as subtle as an elephant about it. I plan to talk to him about that."

He chuckled. "I bet you will too. I hope you put them in a safe place."

"There's no combination to get to it, but it's not likely anyone will stumble on to it, either."

I wanted to change the subject. "Michael, doesn't anyone really have any idea where your mother might be?" At the moment it was probably worrying me more than anyone.

He looked sad for just a minute, and then he shrugged. "Mother has been pulling this act for some time. Gramps claims she does it to get Father's attention. If Gramps is right, it usually works. You'd think after about twenty years of it. . . ." He shook his head. "She used to tell Mrs. Kiley when she was leaving, but she stopped that years ago. I'll admit, Father never has given her very much attention, at least through the years I've been around." He smiled thinly. "He gives her everything else maybe, but very little of himself."

"Does anyone know where she disappears to?" It seemed a little bizarre to me.

"Gramps used to think she kept an apartment somewhere since she usually takes her dog. She's always had a little poodle. My father thinks she just goes to a hotel or motel where they allow little dogs. Mother refuses to say where she's been. She claims it's her prerogative." He smiled. "Of course, she's right, but we did at one time think she should account for herself much more closely than any of us wanted to account for ourselves. Kind of one-way, I'll admit. Anyway, when she returns, she only asks if anyone missed her. It's kind of a family catch phrase."

"You said that when you arrived, didn't you?" He nodded. "Your mother always seems so . . . vulnerable to me. Until this morning, that is. She appeared to be quite in charge after the explosion."

Michael was doing a good job of getting my clothes picked up and put on hangers. Nothing was very wrinkled, thankfully. "Don't let Mother fool you," he said. "She's an intelligent woman and very self-sufficient. That foggy act she puts on most of the time is one I think she got good reviews on from my father once, and she's never given it up. Believe me, Mother can take care of herself and anyone else if the need occurs." He smiled proudly.

"I think I'll go talk to Barney and see if he heard her leave this morning," he continued. "It's a little out of character for her to leave so soon after I arrive home. In fact, she hasn't pulled this sort of thing when I've been home since I was in college." He handed me the last of my clothes. "Want to come along?"

I looked around the room. The messy dressing table could wait. "Yes, I would." I wasn't sure I was ready for yet another mystery, but I was concerned for Emily Kincade. I was only half convinced of her self-sufficiency.

Barney Tully lived over the garage built originally for coaches or wagons. It had been remodeled to hold seven cars. There was also a stall with a lift for cars and a storage room for tools. Barney took care of everyone's car. He also helped either the gardener or Tommy Allen, who lived over the stables and took care of the horses. Of all the employees for the ranch, the gardens, and the house, only Tommy and Barney lived on the ranch besides Mrs. Kiley and Marie Trent. They had all been with the family for many years and, indeed, seemed to be accepted as part of the family.

Barney was walking up to the garage from the stables when we met him. He was a big, friendly man in his fifties who gave Michael a warm greeting. "How're you doing, Michael, my boy? Heard you'd come home. Think it's time to shake everybody up again?" He laughed heartily and winked at me.

Michael laughed with him as they shook hands vigorously. "Something like that, Barney. Dropped by to see you this morning, but Tommy told me you'd gone to church. Still trying to redeem yourself on Sunday for your treachery all week, I see."

Barney's shoulders shook with laughter. "You bet. I'm not taking any chances."

Michael looked at the array of cars. One stall was empty. "Barney, did you hear my mother leave this morning?"

The older man's face sobered while he shook his

head from side to side. "Nope, I didn't. I know she left pretty early. After that explosion this morning— Well, I came back and went to bed. I guess I slept like a log. I had my alarm set for before seven so I could make eight-o'clock mass. I let it go off a couple of times before I got up. I guess it was about quarter to eight when I came out to go to church. Her car was gone then." He scowled.

Michael looked off at the corral. Barney leaned back against the garage and shoved his hands into his pockets. "It's kind of strange she'd disappear again so soon, and with you home and all, Michael." He took a deep breath. "Usually about three months pass between her disappearing acts. And I don't remember her being gone when you've been home since you started traveling. Always felt you were her favorite." He chuckled softly. "She comes down here, and we have long talks once in a while. She envies you, you know, since you started your roaming. Anyway, she disappeared for a week just before Laura moved in." He looked over at me. "Wasn't that about a month ago?"

"Yes, it was. This is my fourth weekend here."

Barney laughed softly. "That lady knows how to shake everyone up. I guess you get your restless feet from her, Michael."

Michael asked the question that was on my mind. "Have you seen Uncle Harvey this morning?"

"Yeah, he came down right after I got home from church. I guess that was maybe about eleven o'clock." Barney chuckled. "I guess he and Jason had been at it. He was muttering about these blasted kids who can't think."

"They're still at it, I see," Michael said. "They used to argue a lot even when Jason was a teenager. Mother said it was because Harvey didn't understand kids, since he didn't have any. Also, Jason had a very quick mind, and he was always impatient with Harvey's roundabout way of getting to a point." He looked at me. "Do they argue a lot at the office?"

I nodded.

"Harvey tinkered with his car for a while this morning," Barney went on. "I helped him a little, but there really wasn't much wrong with it. Harvey's always been pretty good at tinkering with electrical things and that sort, but he's never learned much about engines." He pointed down the driveway. "His car's down there, ready to go. He's up at the house now. Said he had to get something. Then I guess he's on his way. I told him I thought his nerves were getting bad, and he said mine would, too, if I had to put up with what he had to put up with."

Although we received no enlightening information concerning the present whereabouts of Emily from Barney, I felt I was further enlightened about her. Except for her flighty manner, Emily Kincade was the one person in the family I would never have thought had any really secretive, quirky ways. I was never one-hundred-percent sure of anyone else. As we walked back to the house in silence, I did a quick amateur analysis of the flaws of this family I was beginning to feel so much a part of.

I knew J.B. was sharp, domineering, and temperamental. I didn't try to guess what else he might be. His secret phone calls suggested something going on that he didn't want on the front page of the paper. Well, most of us might have that sort of thing going on in our lives, and it could be next to nothing.

Amanda was haughty and, as my grandmother would say, full of herself. She was vain to the point of the ridiculous and really gave very little thought to anything beyond her next manicure appointment or her next party.

Gramps was a love, but I had learned he was a highly suspicious man who felt everyone had a bent side, as he called it.

Jason had a secretive side to him, all right. He had no idea how many times I'd seen him or his car in a place that did not suggest he lived for research and development.

Kyle was conceited and lazy and proud that he had never earned a dime in his life. That was J.B.'s evaluation. However, he didn't appear lethal in any way. And there was something about Kyle that didn't ring right with J.B.'s opinion, but it was one of the many things around there I couldn't put my finger on. He didn't appear all that conceited or lazy or proud to me, but what did I know?

I guess one could say Michael was the most secretive of all. His entire adult life was a mystery to all. It was so asinine of him, unless, of course, he had a darn good reason. Was he into something illegal? I brushed the thought aside and turned my thoughts back to Emily.

The worst I ever thought of Emily Kincade was that she might be a flake. Putting together what Michael had said about his mother and what Barney had just said about her, I wondered.

A telephone rang as we stepped through the front door. We hung our jackets on the rack in the foyer and turned to go to the kitchen. J.B.'s voice roared from his room. "Who's that?"

Michael glanced down at me before he turned toward his father's room, yelling back at him. "It's Laura and Michael. What's your problem, Dad?"

The door to J.B.'s bedroom was ajar, and Michael pushed it open. I came up behind him and saw J.B. sitting in his big chair, with the phone in one hand. He shouted at us, "You two get on the phone in the office. Someone says they have your mother, but they want someone else to hear their instructions. They want to be sure Laura gets the message right, they say."

His face was red, and his eyes were flashing. I held my breath. He looked as though he might be on the verge of an attack or something. I wondered where Kyle might be.

We raced into my office, and Michael grabbed the phone, holding it so I could hear what the caller had to say. "This is Michael Kincade," Michael snapped. "Laura Grant is on the phone with us too. What do you have to say?" Although his voice was sharp, Michael was surprisingly calm. I wasn't calm at all. He slipped his arm around my waist. It helped.

The voice on the phone was disguised or garbled. I wasn't sure which. It didn't sound quite human. "Okay, listen. One of you should get this right. We're holding your Emily and will hold her until you give us your copy of the specifications for the Hardcase project. We want the ones Watson & Company gave you without any editing by any of you."

The hesitation sounded odd, and it occurred to me this whole thing could be a recording. I looked up at Michael, who was frowning. J.B. broke the silence. "Now you listen here, whoever you are. We can't—"

The voice on the other end of the line interrupted him. "We didn't expect your approval, but if you want your Emily back, you'd better get the specifications to us. We want Laura Grant to bring them out to the windmill on Cutter Hill."

"That's a dead-end road out there," J.B. said. "She'd be—"

Again the voice cut him off. "We didn't expect you to be thrilled about that, either, but that's the way it will have to be. She's to take the cutoff for Cutter Hill, take the first dirt road after the cutoff, and drive two miles. She's not a member of the family, but she's the only one in that house we trust. She could split and run out on all of us, but believe me, we'll have her under surveillance from the minute she leaves the house until she arrives at the windmill. If she splits, we'll be able to overtake her in a short time, and she'll be one sorry girl. We don't want to see anyone else. Do you understand?"

J.B. started to speak during the silence, but Michael stopped him. "Dad, forget it. We're listening to a tape."

The voice came back. "If Laura Grant won't do it, everything's off. You won't see Emily again, and we'll find another way to get those specs that you may find even less to your liking. We'll leave a red box at the base of the windmill. Tomorrow morning at six o'clock Laura Grant is to place the specs in the box and leave immediately. We'll pick up the specs, get them verified, and then, if they're the right ones, we'll send Emily home. We'll know if they're the right ones, believe me. Laura is to be on time, and she is to be alone. Does everyone understand?" The short silence that followed was broken by a click.

CHAPTER FIVE

MICHAEL had a tight grip on the phone. He looked at it for a minute before he slammed the receiver down. His skin had turned dark red and was drawn tightly over his jaw. His blue eyes looked more like hot steel than the afternoon sky. A chill ran through me. In the next room, J.B. was yelling into the phone. Michael stepped to the door. "Forget it, Father. I've broken the connection."

I followed Michael into J.B.'s room. Michael stood straight, his hands on his hips, and looked out the window for a minute. Then he dropped his eyes to his father's. "I'm having a tap put on all the phones in this house. Laura will not make that delivery in the morning."

"But your mother—" I said.

J.B. sat upright. "What do you mean, a tap? I don't want the police brought into this."

Michael stopped him. "Look, this concerns my mother." His voice was cold and steady. "He won't harm Mother if Laura doesn't show tomorrow. He needs both women. He knows Laura and he trusts

66

her. And he wants those specs. When Laura doesn't show in the morning, he'll have to call back to set another time. This time we'll trace the call and make sure he lets us talk to Mother. Whoever called just now wanted to drop the bomb, so to speak. He didn't say anything other than his demands so as not to spoil the effect. However, tomorrow he'll be angry and I'm sure will have plenty to say." He looked down at me. "Are you willing to go through with whatever charade he wants?"

Michael Kincade was now a totally different man. I felt a little in awe of him. He was very much in charge and very authoritative. There was a no-nonsense air about him, where just such a short time ago he seemed to be full of mischief. I wanted to ask him just who the real Michael Kincade might be, but didn't. Instead, I said, "Of course I will."

Michael nodded with approval. "Good. I assure you I'll find a way to give you protection." He left the room.

J.B. frowned. "I don't think I know my firstborn son at all," he said.

I understood what he meant. Michael walked across the foyer and into the library. He picked up a phone that was well out of our hearing range.

J.B. and I watched Michael talking on the phone for a few minutes without saying a word to each other. I'd like to have heard what Michael was saying, and I'm sure J.B. would have also, but we were both above listening in on an extension. Although there were several phone numbers for the ranch, they were all interconnected, with the exception of the private line in J.B.'s room and the one in Tommy Allen's room above the stable. There was also an intercom line on each instrument to call anyone else in the house. Each phone was a mini-switchboard as far as I was concerned.

I turned my attention back to the shaken man in the chair beside me. I wished I knew just what to do for him. His face was ashen. There was, however, something I wanted him to know. "J.B.," I began, "while we're alone, I want to tell you where I put the specs. I didn't know if you had a specific place in mind when you gave them to me, but I put them—"

He raised his hand. "I didn't have any place in mind. I knew you'd think of something when I gave you that envelope. Don't tell me yet. I don't want to let anything slip. It's painful enough to know that someone in my family, or connected with my family, is involved in all this. The fact that they're so unconscionable as to hold Emily makes me shudder." He patted my hand. "As long as you're the only one who knows where the envelope is, we know it's safe."

A dead weight landed on my chest. "If that's the way you want it, J.B. But may I ask why you waved that envelope around so obviously in front of Kyle this morning?" I couldn't keep my annoyance out of my voice.

"I wanted him to see it and know I'd given it to you. I don't suspect Kyle of anything. He's too busy being dedicated to the pursuit of pretty women to get involved in a covert affair involving theft." He rolled his eyes to the ceiling. "I'd be very much surprised to know that our Kyle even knows what a specification might be. I just wanted him to see it in case someone asked him if he knew where it was. I wanted him to know we had it and it was going to be put away."

I wanted to say, "Thanks a lot." What he let Kyle know was that I had the specifications. Kyle had told Amanda, Michael said. Who knows where the information went from there? It went to someone who thought I might be dumb enough to hide it in my room. I still thought J.B. should know where I stashed the envelope. "J.B., I do think you should—"

He held up his hand again to stop me. "We'll talk about it some other time. Do you happen to know who is away from the ranch right now?"

I tried to think. "I saw Harvey drive out just as Michael and I came in the front door. That was just before you called to us. The last time I saw Amanda and Ralph Satterly, they were going to the kitchen for the hot chocolate she had started before we found my room ransacked. Mrs. Kiley is next door at the Sunrise ranch with a pecan pie for Mr. Fitzgerald's eightieth birthday. Gramps and Marie usually take their naps this time of day." I shrugged. "I don't know where Kyle and Jason are."

He smiled. "You're always so efficient."

"Isn't she, though?" Jason said as he walked into the room. "Jason's right here. Why does anyone care?"

"Your mother is missing," I said softly.

He raised an eyebrow. "What else is new?"

I flinched. It sounded so callous.

He walked over beside me, slipped his arm around my waist, and spoke in a confidential tone. "I just passed the library door. My big brother is in there on the phone and talking in a very hush-hush voice. He told someone, 'I've given you everything I have. When I get more, I'll let you know. Take care of this immediately. It will be greatly appreciated.' " Jason's smug expression was very much out of character for this man of little emotion.

J.B. sighed wearily. "He's having a tap put on all our phones."

Jason dropped his arm from my waist. "He's doing what?"

"He's having wiretaps put on our phones. We've had a call about ransom for your mother. They want the Hardcase specs for her return."

"Who put him in charge?" Jason looked back toward the foyer. There was real anger in his eyes. A new side to Kincade Industries' Prince Charming was showing.

J.B. glared at his younger son for a moment and then spoke in a monotone. "He took charge himself, and I approve."

Jason narrowed his eyes. "You approve? Don't you think we can handle this ourselves?" he asked. "You said you didn't want law enforcement in on this. It's likely a family affair. Isn't the law who he's talking to?"

J.B. shook his head. He looked very drawn and tired. I was about to take Jason's arm and pull him out of the room. J.B. spoke first. "I know what I said," he said curtly, "but I'm going to let Michael run the show."

"Why, for heaven's—" Jason's voice came as close to shouting as I'd ever heard out of him.

J.B. narrowed his eyes. His face was totally without emotion. "Because I say so, that's why."

Jason took in a deep, exasperated breath and let it out loudly. He looked at me and then placed his hands on his hips and spoke to his father in a tone much like one he might use with a difficult child. "Now, Father, how do you know he's not behind it all? He doesn't care what goes on around here. He stays away for months and years at a time. He was away over two years this last time. He certainly doesn't care anything about Kincade Industries. I think he's the most likely suspect of any of us. We have no idea what he does for a living or what his talents are these days or what associations he may have developed. Putting him in charge is right next to putting the fox in charge of the chicken coop."

The grayness of J.B.'s skin alarmed me. I laid my hand firmly on Jason's arm and spoke sharply. "Jason, I think we'd better let J.B. get some rest. He's had a very upsetting day, and I, for one, don't want to see him upset further." I dug my fingers into his arm.

To my surprise, J.B. broke into a thin smile. "Look, Jason, just because you didn't get your own way about closing the office here, there's no reason for you to spend the rest of the day spoiling for a fight. I've told you for years, no one wins them all. I'm afraid you take after your Uncle Harvey in that you can't bear not to win all the time. It's one of the reasons Father has always told Harvey he's not cut out to run the firm. He's too rigid. He expects too much from everyone. He's never ready to shift into another gear if the road changes. In essence, he never has a Plan B. People must believe as he does or they're wrong and he wants them to pay for it."

Jason let out an exasperated sigh. "Now, Father—"

J.B. cut him off. "Now, you wait, Jason. I have something to say here." He glanced across the foyer at Michael in the library and then looked up at Jason. I had an uncanny feeling he wasn't crazy about either of his sons. Maybe I could understand Michael being in bad standing, but Jason did pretty much just as J.B. wanted him to do from what I could tell.

I looked at the two men and narrowed my eyes at J.B. "J.B., you need some rest."

He glanced at me and nodded. "Yes, yes, in just a minute." He looked back at Jason. "I believe Michael never heard of the Hardcase project before the explosion this morning. Whoever wants those specs is going too far. They're holding your mother, and they want Laura to bring the specs out to them at the windmill on Cutter Hill at six in the morning. It's isolated out there, and there's only one road that goes back to that windmill. It's still dark at that hour of the morning this time of year. Michael thinks he can protect her. There is more here, Jason, than your sibling rivalry with Michael that has been going on since you two became aware of each other."

"But what if Michael is involved?" Jason asked.

At that moment Amanda started carrying on in the foyer like a banshee. That wasn't unusual, but I didn't know what had set her off until Michael showed up in the doorway, with a twisted grin. I felt the old Michael had returned.

"I just told Amanda to call off her party tonight," he said. "I've told Mrs. Kiley to cancel the caterer. I don't want anyone to bother the guys who will be working on our phone lines." He frowned at Jason. "I suppose you know by now."

"Yes, I do. I think you should know, Michael, that, in my opinion, you may be the best suspect we have. We had no problem with the specs for Hardcase until you arrived home."

Michael smiled again. "I guess we're both starting at square one, little brother. I feel very strongly that you and/or Uncle Harvey are probably our most logical suspects."

I'd had enough. I stepped between them. "Okay, boys," I said firmly, "your bickering isn't going to accomplish a thing. We aren't going to get anywhere accusing each other. Until we know who the culprit is, let's act like adults, shall we?" I glared from one to the other, letting my gaze rest on Michael. "When are the men coming to work on the phones?"

It rather surprised me that no one took exception to my outburst. In fact, J.B. smiled just slightly. Michael looked at his watch. "In about an hour."

I looked out the window at the rain splattering against the pane. Sometime during all this, the sky had darkened considerably and promised a stormy night. I stood up and took a deep breath. "Okay, gentlemen, out." I shooed them ahead of me with my hands. "It's time we left J.B. alone and let him get some rest. Does anyone happen to know where Kyle might be?" It occurred to me I hadn't seen him since he helped straighten my room. The door to his room was open, but he wasn't in there.

No one knew Kyle's whereabouts. We all filed out of J.B.'s room as he raised the footrest on his recliner and flicked on his TV with a remote control. That combination usually allowed him to rest quite well.

I helped Mrs. Kiley set out a buffet dinner. Gramps and Marie Trent took their meals in their rooms. Gramps took our phone call for ransom much too lightly, I thought. He whispered to Marie and me that maybe Emily had staged this herself and had a boyfriend who wanted the specs. He laughed, but I wasn't sure he was kidding. I couldn't buy that.

Amanda and Ralph fixed their plates and disappeared into the library. Ralph was leaving at dawn, I heard. It was hoped the downpour would have passed by then. I took a tray into J.B. In general, I tried to stay out of the way.

The men working on the phones were invited to fix their own plates and sit at the dining-room table. They had arrived in two matching, nondescript, older, gray Ford sedans. Jason commented to me on the fact. Although it seemed a bit odd to me also, I merely shrugged. None of them said much to any of us. They were polite but gave only one-word answers to questions or suggested we see Michael for answers. Michael was definitely in charge of everything. Again I wondered just who the real Michael Kincade might be. The time was near when I knew I'd ask him just that. Maybe. He seemed so much more formidable now.

I watched the men work on the phones in J.B.'s room and my office. Dressed in casual clothes, they ranged in age between their late twenties and late forties. I wanted to ask who they were, but I didn't. Something made me a little apprehensive, but I couldn't be sure what was doing it. My nerves felt stretched. Jason didn't help anything. He roamed around like an uneasy panther.

After I ate half a chicken sandwich, I took a cup of coffee and wandered into my office and stood by the French doors to watch the rain. The blackness of the night allowed little to be seen beyond the terrace.

Michael came up beside me. "You okay, Laura?"

I turned and looked up at him with a feeble smile. "Yes, I guess so. I think everything is beginning to overwhelm me a little."

He slipped his arm around my waist and pulled me to him. The gesture surprised me, as did the light kiss he dropped on my forehead. "The day has been a strain for all of us." He squeezed my waist slightly, and I let my body lean into his. It felt good to have him so close. He was able both to excite me and to calm me by just being near. It wasn't something I was used to. I'm not sure anyone had ever had that much control over me. I wasn't even sure I liked it, but I didn't want him to move away from me, either.

I looked up at his face in the dim light. He gazed out into the darkness and started talking without looking at me. "When a new time is set for delivering the specs, I want you to drive J.B.'s Lincoln. It has the biggest backseating area of any car in the garage. I'll crouch down on the floor behind you. I can't let you go out there alone, and that's all there is to it. Just watching you from afar wouldn't do it for me." He squeezed my waist gently and glanced down at me with a faint smile.

I returned his smile, not wanting to admit how much better his idea made me feel. However, I'd be alone with him, and I'd have the specs. If he was the one or if he was involved with those who wanted the specs. . . . I didn't finish that thought. Instead, I asked him a question that had been bothering me. "Michael, were you serious when you said you suspected Jason?"

"Yes. I've never fully trusted Jason—or Uncle Harvey, either, for that matter."

"But why would he do it, for heaven's sake? Jason is an officer of Kincade Industries. He'd profit from the success of Kincade Industries' involvement with the Hardcase project. Why would he want to steal it or help anyone steal it? I can't think of a motive for him."

His laughter was deep. "I bet you could think of a motive for me."

"Well, I don't know. No one knows anything about you. But Jason. . . ."

"Ah, yes, Jason, the son every woman wants. But our dutiful Jason could have been offered a very lucrative deal if he would liberate the specs from Kincade Industries. If successful, maybe he could even liberate himself from the nepotism of Kincade Industries."

I frowned. "That seems a bit farfetched to me. I think Jason enjoys his job." I suddenly realized I was out of my league. I didn't know Jason well enough to know how he felt about his job or Kincade Industries or even his father. One of the men working on the phones called Michael.

After Michael left my side, I tried to think just what I did know about Jason Kincade. We'd had a lot of togetherness both at the office when I worked with him on the Sommer's project and during the past month on the ranch when we rode out into the forest for picnic lunches. But, as I thought about it, I didn't know him well from things he said about himself. I did, however, know a little bit about his life that I felt sure he thought he kept quite secret.

One night, when I was on a date with Jack Burns, his brother, Nick, and his wife joined us. Nick said he wanted to show Jack and me a place we'd probably never visited. We drove to Blackie's Roadhouse. It was only a few blocks from my apartment building. I'd passed it many times, but I'd never been inside.

It sat back from the road and was nearly hidden by trees. The lounge was tastefully decorated with a Western decor, but, with Nick using his influence or whatever, we were allowed into the back room. It was lush, with red carpeting, red-and-gold-flocked wallpaper, and gilded chandeliers. It tended to resemble one of the casinos on the Las Vegas Strip. It was smoky and crowded with well-dressed men and women. Sitting at a baccarat table, oblivious to the people around him, was Jason, with a large stack of chips in front of him.

Jack and I watched his brother and his wife play twenty-one, and we played a few slot machines, but after a short time we left. In California gambling is illegal, and it made me nervous just being there. I kept one eye on Jason during our stay, and I've always been sure he didn't see me. ˊ

After that I noticed his distinctive yellow Porsche in that parking lot many evenings when I passed by Blackie's Roadhouse on the way home. Also, a classmate of mine who, with her husband, ran a fine jewelry store at one of the big hotels in Las Vegas had seen Jason in that casino many times. Jason's outstanding good looks made it very difficult for him to fade into the background anywhere.

I remembered what Michael had said about Jason's selfishness. I had trouble buying that one. Maybe we didn't have a relationship that spawned candlelight dinners, unexpected flowers, or flashes of lightning magic, but I felt we did know each other well enough that I would detect selfishness if it were there. Jason had always been generous with his time and his knowledge at the office.

Michael returned and interrupted my thoughts. I looked up at him and realized that he and Jason really didn't look alike at all. Both were breathtakingly handsome men, but except for the color and size of their eyes, they bore little resemblance. At that moment I would have said Michael had the edge. I immediately decided I was more tired than I had realized. I hardly knew the man, and already I had the strong feeling I was falling in love with him.

I was just starting up the stairs to bed when Kyle came in the front door. Jason, who by far had the edge on temperament that night, as out of character as it was for him, jumped on Kyle before he'd hung up his coat. "Where have you been?"

Kyle frowned, but a grin played around his mouth. "I didn't know you cared, Jason, but I've been with my dad most of the day. He hasn't been feeling too well."

With J.B., Michael, Jason, and Kyle, I was by the phone at six the next morning. Michael didn't doubt we'd have another call as soon as six o'clock came and went and it was realized I wasn't going to show at Cutter Hill. It was seven-thirty when the phone rang. J.B. let each of us get to different phones before he answered. This time it wasn't a recording. The voice was garbled as before, but it was easy to tell it was a very angry man, in person. "Okay, Kincade.

What happened? You want to get rid of your wife or something? Where's Laura Grant and the specs?"

Following Michael's directions, J.B. held the phone receiver to the tape player and turned it on. "This is J.B. Kincade, Junior. I will not allow the specifications for Hardcase to be out of my possession until I speak with my wife. If this condition is not met, then I will not release the specifications. Please state when I may hear her voice. This is a recording."

The man let out a line of obscenities. When he finished that bit, he spoke harshly into the phone. "You listen to this, J.B. Kincade, Junior. You'll see and hear your wife when I say, and that will be after I get the specs and have them verified. Do you hear that, old man? You'd better, because your wife's future is in your hands. You get that Laura Grant out to Cutter Hill at nine o'clock tonight. It's the last offer you're going to get."

J.B. hesitated and Michael spoke up. "You'd better not hurt that woman. Believe me, I'll find you. I'm Michael Kincade."

The man laughed, but it wasn't a happy sound. "I know who you are, Michael Kincade, but you won't find us. You'd better get that Grant girl out here tonight if you ever want to see your mommy again. Believe me, none of you out there will like our other options nearly as well. We *will* get the specs." The man hung up.

I frowned at Michael. "That was a real man that time, not a recording. His voice was so garbled it was hard to tell anything about him." I was half talking to myself. "Isn't he taking a chance, setting the time and place up so far ahead of time again? Couldn't we have it surrounded with police?"

Jason walked into the office and answered my question. "Cutter Hill isn't really a hill. It's a mound of earth in a small clearing with a plaque on top. It's an old Indian burial ground. However, it's surrounded by a thick stand of trees that goes on, over rugged land, for some distance. It would take the Army to cover it all. These guys know that."

I digested that information. It didn't make me feel any easier. I remembered that man had said he knew Michael. I wished I knew Michael better.

Jason pulled me aside. "Laura, I hate it that they've involved you in this. I don't like the idea of you going out there to these people we don't know." He picked up my hand and squeezed it.

Kyle called to us from J.B.'s room. "Somebody call the doctor. I think J.B. is having another stroke."

CHAPTER SIX

WHILE I called J.B.'s doctor, with great effort Michael, Jason, and Kyle got J.B. into the backseat of his Lincoln. It was not an easy task, especially with Mrs. Kiley and Marie Trent giving them advice. Marie, being a practical nurse, gave Michael welcomed instructions for J.B.'s care on the trip. Michael sat in back with him; Kyle drove. Jason wanted to take his own car, and I rode with him. We were quiet most of the way, trying to control our nerves, I guess.

Sitting in the waiting room, we all thumbed through old magazines, drank coffee, and tried to act calm. If I didn't know it before, I learned that morning that these men had difficulty saying a civil sentence to each other. Childish as it seemed, it was a fact. Thankfully, after the first hour they rarely spoke.

After the second hour of sitting in that small room, waiting to hear some word of J.B.'s condition, I jumped up. "I'm going to take a short walk. I'm not good at the waiting game."

Jason leaped to his feet. "I'll go with you." Michael looked up from his magazine, frowned, but didn't move. Jason said, "We'll be out on the side lawn." He took my elbow and ushered me out of the room. When we got outside, he let out a long breath. "A place like that is stifling."

"I noticed. Oh, Jason, I'm so worried about your father!" I looked up at him and tried to smile. "You know, he's become a little more than my boss these last few weeks. He's. . . ." I shrugged. I didn't want to sound maudlin.

Jason picked up my hand and squeezed it. "I know what you mean. He grows on one. I know for a fact you've become much more than an employee to him also. You're much more than that to all of us." He smiled as he squeezed my hand again. "Whether you want us or not, you've become family"—he narrowed his eyes playfully—"and more."

I swallowed the lump in my throat. If he had said that a week ago, looked at me like that and squeezed my hand, all at the same time, it would have certainly made my heart beat faster. Right then it just made me feel good. I wondered about that, but only for a minute. We walked along the side of the building and down a walk through a beautiful garden. "This is lovely."

Jason looked around. "It is, at that. I never paid much attention." He hesitated and then went on as though carefully thinking out his words. "Laura, I've noticed you spent some of the day yesterday with Michael. Remember, I warned you he can't be trusted.

I think he can be dangerous. None of us has ever had the slightest idea what kind of life-style he has. He comes home wearing very good clothes, driving an expensive car, and telling grandiose tales of his world travels. He describes in vivid detail the culture of people in exotic places without one word of explanation about why he happened to be there."

"Doesn't anyone ever question him?"

"Oh, yes. Father, Kyle, and I have all asked him just how he happens to be in these places and how he lives." He looked down at me with a deep scowl. "He says he enjoys seeing how the other half gets along, and he lives day by day and does it very well. That's the only answer he ever gives anyone," he said in disgust.

I laughed lightly. I could just hear Michael saying that. "That's really all he says?"

"Yep. Father has pushed him for an answer, but he won't say, and I know he enjoys everyone's frustration. He reminds Father that he stays out of jail and the newspapers and has never asked for a dime since he left college and law school. He also has reminded us from time to time that he paid part of his own way through both by working and the rest was paid by his inheritance from our Grandmother Kincade."

Jason frowned. "All four of us received the same inheritance on our eighteenth birthday. Michael used his for his education. The rest of us blew ours, I'm afraid. Amanda, Kyle, and I lived it up through college much more than Dad would have paid for and, of course, much more than brother Michael."

We stopped at a small pond with concrete benches. Jason sat down and pulled me down beside him.

"Well, it's probably his way of asserting his independence," I said. My armchair psychology aside, I wondered why I was defending Michael. I suspected why, but I still wondered why I would do it with Jason.

"One reason he brings up the fact that he paid for his own education when he gets pushed about his lifestyle is that neither Kyle nor I worked until our senior year. The summer between my junior and senior year, I did work at Kincade Industries. In Kyle's senior year Gramps had the stroke that put him in that chair. Kyle helped tend him that year and all through the next summer. Of course, Kyle never has held a regular job in the ten years since he finished college. Michael started working summers and vacations in an attorney's office in his sophomore year."

I wondered how much of all this information, being said in a voice touched with acid, was merely part of the lifelong sibling rivalry J.B. alluded to. "What did Michael major in at college?"

"I don't know. He went to law school, so he's a lawyer, but obviously not so one would notice. I've checked. Nowhere in this country is there a Michael James Kincade who practices law that any bar association knows about."

It was definitely time to change the subject. I stood

up. "Let's walk." It seemed a splendid idea. I could bet Jason was grinding his teeth.

Jason stood up and picked up my hands. "By the way, Laura, I don't think anyone's said thank you for coming along today. We need you with us, if for no other reason than to keep us away from each other's throat."

"Have you three ever gotten along?"

"No, not really. We've never been friends although we're all close in age. We've tolerated each other because of blood. I guess both Michael and I can stand Kyle longer than we can stand each other. Right now I suspect Michael of being involved in the Hardcase thing, but I'm not absolutely sure Kyle isn't involved in some way. We know Michael suspects me, and who knows what goes on in Kyle's mind? I've never believed he's quite as irresponsible and shiftless as he pretends to be." He laughed lightly. "I've thought for years that he leads a double life. I've never mentioned it to anyone because I doubt anyone else would think him capable."

We started walking. How many double lives could there be in this family? Emily disappeared for long spells and didn't tell anyone where she'd been. Michael was a total enigma. I knew Jason gambled a lot, but I doubted anyone else knew. What about J.B. and his long phone calls behind close doors? What about Amanda? Was she, too, not merely the spoiled brat she appeared to be? Did Kyle really have another pursuit other than the one for women that J.B.

thought was his one and only? What a family! What about Harvey?

We strolled along in silence, and I lost myself in thought. It was amazing that I wasn't more thrilled with Jason's attentions, with the fact that he was confiding these family intimacies or whatever to me. For nearly three years I laughed at myself because I had fantasized about this man. True, I did recognize it as fantasy, but during that time the man could have definitely turned my head, as my mother would say.

Jason broke into my thoughts by stepping in front of me and smiling down at me. "Laura, when this is all over, I feel very strongly that the time will be right for you and me to have a long, serious discussion. I think we have a lot in common. I think we've gotten to know each other a lot better during this past month, and I think we've both enjoyed it. I think—"

A nurse stepped out of the hospital side door and called to us. "Mr. Kincade"—she waved her hand, beckoning us—"Dr. Stuart wants to talk to you and your family."

We raced up the hill to the hospital. When we reached the waiting room, Amanda was there and Dr. Stuart was talking. "We've put J.B. into intensive care. We won't know how bad this is for some time. He hasn't regained consciousness yet, but that's not necessarily a bad sign at this point. J.B. is a healthy man in general, and I'm very optimistic. I don't see any reason for any of you to stay around here. We'll call you if there is any change."

*   *   *

It was after three o'clock when we arrived back at the ranch. After we reported to Mrs. Kiley and Gramps and Marie Trent, we went to clean up. Since I had gotten up before five, I had only splashed my face with water and pulled on the same clothes I'd worn the day before. And my hair was a mess. It had rained off and on all day.

I expected a great deal from my shower. I wanted it to revive me, to lift my spirits, to take away the numbness I felt. I also hoped it would at least alleviate some of the apprehension building in me concerning the trip I had to take to Cutter Hill. As the time grew closer, the thought of that trip made my blood run cold.

After I dried off, I pulled on a terry robe and walked over to the window. At one time, I'd been told, large herds of cattle had been run on the Kincade ranch. Now, after much of the land had been sold off, it could be called a gentleman's ranch. There were no more cattle. Now they bred horses. The horses were from good stock, according to Gramps, and there was always a waiting market for them. It was a beautiful place, with gently rolling land dotted with oak and poplar trees. To the east, tall old pine trees ran endlessly up the mountainside.

The house was old but as modern and elegant, without being pretentious, as any modern house. The grounds around the house were neat, but the gardener, somehow, had been able to hold on to more than enough of the natural growth to allow the squirrels, birds, and deer to feel at home.

I turned away from the window and fell across the bed. The shower had failed to revive me, and I realized I was dead tired. I reviewed what Jason had said about Kyle. I couldn't form an opinion about the possibility of Kyle's leading a double life. If he did, he did a great job of hiding it. Maybe he wasn't as cavalier as he appeared.

My mind jumped to the conversation with Jason at the hospital. He'd said he thought we'd gotten to know each other quite well during this past month. Maybe he'd gotten to know me better, but I wasn't sure I knew him much better. I'd seen many sides to him I hadn't seen before. I'd learned that though he was a man who had a reputation of having no patience with temperament in anyone, he did have a temper himself.

Of course, I had enjoyed our time together. It did surprise me that some of the magic of his company seemed dimmer. As far as our having a lot in common, I wasn't sure. We both liked to ride, and we were both devoted employees of Kincade Industries. Beyond that. . . .

The next thing I knew, Michael was shaking my shoulder. "Hey, Laura, it's five o'clock. You'd better get dressed and have something to eat before we take off on our little voyage tonight." He leaned over and dropped a light kiss on my chin.

I wanted to reach up and pull him to me, but I let my blasted good sense prevail. I sat up and pulled my robe together. "I didn't know I'd drift off. I'll be down in just a few minutes. Any news from the hospital?"

He shook his head. "I called just a few minutes ago but was told there was no change. I'm not sure how that makes me feel." He started to leave but turned back. "By the way, our phone call this morning came from a pay phone at a gas station in town."

"Great."

"Yeah."

Our light dinner was a quiet affair. Everyone stayed with his own thoughts for the most part after we discussed the weather and the fact that no matter how many times the tape of the phone call that morning was played back, at all different speeds, the voice on the other end of the line did not become any clearer.

When I went upstairs to get my bag and my jacket, Michael waited for me in my open doorway. He slipped his arms around my waist and pulled me to him. He looked down into my eyes for a moment before he spoke. "Laura, are you sure you're up to this now?"

I worked on a smile. "Of course, Michael. How could I not want to do this? They have your mother."

"You're a wonderful and brave woman, Laura Grant. I'm so glad I've met you at this time in my life." He leaned down and surprised me with a kiss. When he raised his head, he smiled down at me. "I'd like to say that's for luck tonight, but it isn't. It was just for me."

I wanted to say, "And for me," but I didn't. I stepped back. "We'd better get the specifications," I said. At the mention of the specs, the spell was broken, and a lump formed in my throat. I wasn't prepared to feel very at ease with those specs on my person. If Jason or Michael were involved. . . . I tried to put that thought out of my mind but only half succeeded.

Michael pulled me to him and kissed me lightly again. He raised his lips and looked into my eyes for a long moment. "That was for me too," he said softly. I wasn't sure I was up to that. He dropped his arms from around my waist and picked up my hand. "Do you want to go after the specs alone, to protect your hiding place?" He was having better luck with a smile than I.

"No. In fact, I can use your height." I took him to the kitchen. Jason fell in behind us when we reached the bottom of the stairs. Jason and Mrs. Kiley watched as I directed Michael to retrieve the specs for me. All three of them were surprised at my hiding place. I was rather proud of it.

Mrs. Kiley was proud of me too. "Now there's a smart girl, boys. One of you had better get smart and see it too."

Heat crept up into my face. I narrowed my eyes at Mrs. Kiley, who was beaming. Jason slipped his arm around my shoulders after Michael handed me the big envelope. We walked out into the foyer, and Jason spoke softly into my ear. "Maybe you'd better make sure the specs are there."

"Of course they're here. This envelope is just as your father handed it to me." When we reached the foyer, I looked at his concerned face. "Okay, I'll open it."

I was glad to see Mrs. Kiley had followed us. It wasn't that I was actually unsure of either Jason or Michael. It was just that I felt better having someone else there as I opened the envelope. I did wonder where Amanda and Kyle had disappeared to. I took out the sheets of paper and laid the envelope on the table in the middle of the foyer. I opened up the sheets of paper and sucked in my breath. I couldn't believe my eyes. I held a handful of blank paper.

I turned and looked from Jason to Michael before I picked up the envelope and inspected it. Both men stared at the blank sheets of paper and frowned deeply. Mrs. Kiley walked over and looked at the papers in my hand after seeing the stunned expressions we all wore. "Now what do you suppose that's all about?"

Michael found his voice first. He turned to Mrs. Kiley. "Has anyone been near that cupboard during the last two days?"

She shook her head. "I think only you and Jason and J.B. could reach it, but no one's been near it, I'm almost sure. It's true, I didn't know Laura had put that thing up there. When did you do that, girl?"

I told her, and she was thoughtful for a minute. "I was out for a while yesterday when I took that pie over to the Sunrise ranch, but I really don't think anyone's been near that cupboard. Would J.B. have a reason to put blank paper in that envelope?"

We looked at each other wordlessly, thinking our own thoughts, and after a moment we all turned and went into J.B.'s room. I didn't know what they were thinking, but I was absolutely furious. Had J.B. hidden the specs somewhere else and made the big production of giving me the envelope so everyone would think I'd hidden them? Why, for heaven's sake? Of course that was why my room was searched. That was probably why Emily's kidnapper wanted me to bring the specs. If J.B. thought that was a clever maneuver, I didn't. I wanted to scream. I wanted to cry. I wanted to hit something.

Kyle came from the library and helped us search J.B.'s room. He gave us his version of just what J.B. had done the morning before. He said J.B. had awakened before he had, but Kyle didn't think J.B. had gotten out of bed. "I think I'd have heard him get up, but I wouldn't bet the ranch on it."

"Can he do that alone?" Jason asked.

"Oh, sure, if he wants to." Kyle shrugged. "After I came in here, we just followed the usual routine to get him bathed and dressed. Then he called Laura in."

I had the men check between the mattress and box spring, where J.B. had had me place the specs. They weren't there. Our search was thorough, but it didn't reveal the specs. We moved to the office and searched it with more thoroughness than a burglar would have done. We found nothing. Why had J.B. done this?

What had he hoped to accomplish? I looked at Kyle. "Could he have hidden them in your room, Kyle? Maybe when you were in the shower or away from the room for whatever reason?"

He shrugged. "I guess anything's possible, but I hardly think it's likely. Come on, let's take a look."

Again the men checked under the mattress. I went through the long dresser while Michael checked the tall chest of drawers and Jason went through Kyle's closet. Mrs. Kiley checked under and around the cushions on the couch and the one chair. Kyle went through his desk, and I did wonder if he was the one who should be doing that. Anyway, we came up empty again.

It was down to the line for me to leave in order to reach Cutter Hill by nine o'clock. We stepped out into the foyer, and I looked up at Michael. "What do I do now? The original set of specs is at the lab, but it would take us more time than we have to get a copy of it. We'd have to go into Sacramento and have Ted Granger meet us at Kincade Industries. Ted, J.B., and Jerry Vacaro, who's on vacation, are the only ones who can open the safe where the specs are kept. We'd have to find Harvey to get his authorization. We'd have to make another copy. It would all take time."

Michael pressed his lips together and looked off over my head. The front door opened, and we turned. A woman came in the door, stamping her wet feet on the mat by the door while taking off her hat. She looked around at our startled faces and smiled. "Hi. Anyone miss me?" It was Emily Kincade.

I grabbed Michael's arm and held on for dear life.

CHAPTER SEVEN

W E surrounded Emily. I'm not sure we didn't frighten her a bit. Jason spoke first. "Mother, where have you been?" He sounded like a cross father chastising his errant child.

She brought Daisy out from under her coat and placed the dog on the floor. Mrs. Kiley helped her with her coat while she looked at us all with an expression that suggested she thought we'd all gone a little mad. "Why, I can't imagine what is the matter with you children. You looked positively shocked to see me. I always do come home, you know." She smiled sweetly.

Michael, with a calmer voice than Jason used, spoke softly. "We have a lot to tell you, Mother. I think we'd better go into the library and sit down." He looked at Mrs. Kiley. "Will you bring us some coffee and then join us?"

Mrs. Kiley nodded and hustled into the kitchen while Michael took his mother's arm and ushered her into the library. The woman was totally bewildered. Jason, Kyle, and I followed. Amanda came down the stairs about then and, after gasping at the sight of her mother, followed us.

Gently Michael told Emily about J.B.'s second stroke. She took it as well as any woman could, I guess. Michael did an excellent job of calming her down. Mrs. Kiley's timing with the coffee was perfect. She poured coffee for all of us and took a chair.

Again gently Michael told his mother of the phone calls. She gasped. "Who do you suppose would do that?"

Michael patted his mother's hand and stood up. He strolled over to the fireplace and leaned against it. "None of us has any idea. You'll never know how relieved we all were to see you come through that door. Mother"—he hesitated a moment and scowled—"I think it might be time, after all these years, for you to tell just where you go when you disappear. During these last two days someone who knows about your disappearing acts played on the fact that no one knows where you go, and we had no defense for it."

Marie and Gramps came in the door while Michael was talking. Gramps didn't act happy to see Emily. "Michael's right, Emily. It's about time you let your little secret out of the bag. You've been pulling these shenanigans long enough. You've had your time in the spotlight, and now it's time you stop worrying everybody. We never know if you've just flown the coop or if you've been hurt or abducted or what. This time it could have cost Kincade Industries dearly."

I resented the way he spoke to Emily. Maybe she

had been foolish through the years, but I didn't think she deserved a dressing-down like that in front of all of us. Of course, it was not my affair, but I still didn't like it. Neither did Emily. She sat forward and narrowed her eyes at him and didn't speak for a minute.

"Well, what do you have to say for yourself?" Gramps demanded.

Emily leaned back in her chair, took a sip of coffee, and looked around at the rest of us, totally ignoring Gramps. I, for one, was glad.

"I think I will tell you children where I spend my time away from here," she said. She smiled at us all, and then she looked at Mrs. Kiley and winked. "I'm sure you'd like to know too, Mrs. Kiley."

Mrs. Kiley laughed. "Oh, indeed, I would, Mrs. Kincade. You wouldn't believe the situations my active imagination has conjured up through the years."

"Oh, I bet I would." Emily set her coffee down, still ignoring Gramps about as obviously as it could be done. "You see, after Amanda started school, life here on the ranch became quite a bore for me. J.B. has been a marvelous provider for all of us, but he has quite set ideas about a wife's role. They are ideas I never did take to.

"Anyway, in those days, he spent most of his time at the office, and there were many days that I was quite sure no one ever even noticed I was here. I decided, therefore, that no one would notice if I wasn't." She raised her eyebrows and smiled mischievously. "The first few years I used to tell Mrs. Kiley I would be gone for a few days. I didn't tell her where

I was going or how long I'd be gone, but at least she knew I was away of my own accord. She had an answer if anyone did happen to miss me." She smiled very sweetly.

Gramps's impatience came to the fore. "Get on with it."

Again she ignored him as she continued her story. "I took an apartment in Sacramento and tried something I had wanted to do since childhood. It was something I knew would get a laugh from both J.B. and Gramps. I bought a typewriter and tried writing."

Amanda came to life. "Writing? What kind of writing?" She sounded angry.

Emily merely smiled. "I write detective stories. I do a lot of plotting and outlining here with pen and paper. When I feel I have quite a lot of notes, I go to the apartment and type it up and do my editing. I have a computer now." She looked at me and smiled. "They are marvelous gadgets, aren't they, Laura?"

"Yes, indeed. Do go on, Mrs. Kincade. I'm dying to hear more."

Emily smiled, but before she could go on, Gramps jumped in. "You mean you've been conjuring up detective stories all these years? What do you do with them?" The look on Gramps's face said he thought it was all preposterous.

"Why, I sell them, Father."

"Sell them?" Now Gramps was shocked. Marie Trent was enjoying his agitation. Gramps sputtered for a moment and then demanded, "Who on earth would buy them from you? You don't know anything about detectives or murder or such."

"Now, Father, I've watched as much TV as anyone, and I've read a lot of books in my day. Anyway, I've been quite successful, I'll have you know."

Kyle spoke up, wearing a pleased grin. "Tell me, Aunt Em, what name do you write under? I buy a lot of detective stories myself. I may know you better in print than I do in person."

"I use two names, actually. Under the name of Paul Savage I write about my detective Clinton Conover. Under the name of Peter Holt my detective is Jason Michaels." She smiled at her two sons.

Michael laughed. "Thank you, Mother. I'm sorry to say I'm not familiar with your heroes."

"Didn't they make a couple of TV movies about both those detectives?" I asked. The names sounded familiar.

"Yes, they did. They did them quite well too."

Amanda leaned forward in her chair, her eyes wide and her mouth open for a moment before she spoke. "Mother, Clinton Conover is a brutal, unethical, coarse man. Jason Michaels is a suave playboy, totally without a conscience, who goes through women just as he does sports cars and expensive clothes. How could you write about such men? You've never known such men, I'm sure."

Emily's smile was almost laughter. "Oh, so you've read some of my books! I do hope they gave you a good read, dear. I had planned to tell you all soon.

I was being forced into it, really. I'm going to receive a very prestigious mystery writer's award next month, and I've finally said I'd give an interview to a man in Los Angeles. My editor has been trying to get me to do it for years but, of course, I wanted to stay anonymous. He's been very good about it, but when I was first nominated for this award, he did think I should open up. When I was informed I had won it, well, I decided he was right."

Michael was grinning broadly since his mother's confession started. Jason was frowning, and Amanda looked petulant. Kyle looked so proud of Emily he could bust. So did Mrs. Kiley. I know I was proud of her. She looked like a pretty little girl who had just won the lead in the school play.

There was a dead silence for a few minutes, so I broke it. "How many books have you written, Mrs. Kincade?"

"Oh, I've written more than I've sold, of course, but in twenty years I've sold over thirty novels."

Gramps made a deep noise in his throat. "They print anything these days. That's the reason I don't read anymore."

Marie laughed. "You don't know what you're missing. I've been half in love with Jason Michaels for years. In a lot of ways he's reminded me of our two handsome boys here." She laughed again and winked at Emily.

Gramps saw none of the humor. He looked up at Michael. "I guess we can stop worrying about giving up the specs." He looked over at me. "I hope you have a good hiding place for them. Come to my room later and tell me where they are. I want to know in case something happens to you." He turned his chair around and left the room calling to Marie.

I watched him leave. I wanted to tell him I had no intention of letting anything happen to me. I also wondered about his dislike for his daughter-in-law, which I had detected so many times. I also wondered about something else. Shouldn't we tell him about the missing specs? I looked up at Michael and spoke softly. "Aren't we going to tell him?"

Michael nodded. "In due time. Excuse me a minute. I've got a phone call to make." He walked over to my office and closed the door.

Emily left the library, with Amanda running after her, still ranting about the kind of books she wrote. Jason and Kyle followed along behind them. Mrs. Kiley cleared away our cups and left.

Alone, I remained in my chair, thinking of Emily and her secret life. Michael returned and took up his seat on the corner of the desk. We were talking about his mother when Kyle returned and joined our conversation.

When Jason walked back into the room, he changed the subject. "Those specs have to be found, you know. Does anyone have any brilliant ideas?"

Kyle answered with my thoughts. "Not a clue, I'm afraid." We all fell into silence, and I realized my nerves were stretched. I wondered if we'd hear from the men who had expected me to drop the specs that night.

It was just ten o'clock when the front door burst open. I jumped. Kyle looked out into the foyer. "Hi, Uncle Harvey, what brings you out here on a night like this?"

After he hung up his coat, Harvey came charging into the library, looking grim. "Do you know your phones are out?"

Michael picked up the phone on the desk and listened to the dial tone. He laid it back down. "It's okay now. I just made a call without a problem. What's wrong?"

"Well, maybe nothing." Harvey lowered his weight into a chair before he continued. "I went by the hospital after I left the office. J.B. is still in intensive care and still unconscious or sedated or something. I tried to call you from there, but the phones were out." He looked up at Jason. "I hope you're planning on coming into the office tomorrow. We've got to make a decision on the Cox matter. J.B. said to hold off on it, but they called today and said they want a yes or no by the end of the week. If we don't give them an answer, they'll take it for a no and find someone else to do their research and development. Do you know why J.B. has wanted to drag his feet on this?"

Jason shrugged. "I don't think he wants any people taken off this Hardcase project. We're spread pretty thin now, you know."

"I don't think that's a worry. It keeps everyone on their toes."

"It also can cut back on their efficiency. I agree with Father on this."

The look on Harvey's face didn't say he was ready to compromise. "We'll talk about it in the morning. You *are* coming in, I presume. It would be nice to have a little help around there." Harvey spoke in that harassed tone we all knew so well.

Jason looked at Michael and, taking turns, they told Uncle Harvey of the events since his departure Sunday afternoon. He had heard only about J.B.'s stroke. After they told him about the phone calls and Emily's secret profession, he let out a long breath and shook his head in disbelief.

Then they told him of the missing specs. He sat forward, blinked his eyes several times, and gasped for air. "What could have happened to them? Where could they be? Who could have stolen them?" He looked at me. "You did check to be sure they were in the envelope when J.B. gave it to you?" He asked it as an accusation.

I took a deep breath and let it out slowly. "No, I didn't. I hardly have reason to question J.B. I put them under his mattress Saturday night after the explosion. That was the last time I actually saw the specs myself." I spoke slowly and distinctly. Harvey had a way of trying my patience with his own impatience. He wanted everything told to him in ten words or less, and he had a nasty habit of blowing sky high if he received an answer he didn't want. Harvey Kincade was not one of my favorite people, but I had learned to get along with him . . . most of the time.

"You should have checked!" he shouted. He remained silent, and for a few minutes no one spoke. I didn't want to say what was on my mind. When Harvey looked up, he narrowed his eyes and looked around at the men. "You know, boys, I've let my mind go to each of you, wondering just how or why any of you might be involved in this whole mess." A slight smile formed on his lips. "I imagine you all have done the same thing since the explosion."

"I'm sure we have, Uncle Harvey," Michael said. "Probably each of us has our own culprit in mind, although I doubt any of us has the same person or any real proof."

Kyle laughed lightly. "Maybe the rest of you have someone in mind, but I'm at a total loss. Frankly, I probably could come up with a possible motive or opportunity for everyone. Maybe we should ask Aunt Em for her opinion. After all, she's the one who solves mysteries."

I laughed. Maybe his idea wasn't all that bad if no one else had any more of a concrete idea than I had. No, I told myself, Emily would hardly have an open mind. She'd never suspect her sons, or her daughter, or her husband, or her nephew. Since she and Gramps were obviously less than friends, she might want to throw suspicion on him, but he couldn't get out of his wheelchair by himself. Besides, it would be hard to find a motive for him, unless it was just to shake everyone up. It was something he might enjoy, but it wasn't likely in this case.

Emily could suspect Harvey, I supposed. Their

hellos and good-byes weren't as friendly as either would give to the new clerk at a store. As I thought about it, I realized I had never seen them in conversation.

Mrs. Kiley, Marie Trent, and Emily were good friends, I'd noticed. Their ages didn't span more than ten years, and they'd lived under the same roof for many, many years. Also, they were the only women around for a good distance, with the exception of Amanda, who, I'd decided, probably wasn't anyone's real friend. Who did that leave? Only the new kid on the block. *Me.* I swallowed the lump in my throat and decided it would be best if no one broached Emily Kincade on the subject.

The grandfather clock chimed eleven o'clock. I stood up. Harvey looked up at me with a smile that didn't look real. "I suppose with all your conjuring for a guilty party, no one has considered Laura. I know her record is spotless, and we all think she's just this side of a genius. However, the phone caller insisted she deliver the specs and—"

"Now wait just a minute, Uncle Harvey—" Jason said as my first defender.

Michael jumped in and interrupted Jason. "From what I understand, she's been cleared to handle your most top-secret matters. She'd hardly have to go through all this. I really don't think we have to worry about Laura." There was annoyance in his voice.

Kyle calmly pointed out I could have gotten away with this particular company treasure anytime with a lot less commotion.

My anger was right there. I waited a moment before I responded to Harvey's accusation. I faced Harvey and narrowed my eyes. "Harvey, I'm going to overlook what you just said for now. I may talk to you about it at length at another time. For what it's worth, I think J.B. put the blank papers in the envelope, gave it to me, and hoped everyone would think I had the specs. He then hid them somewhere he thought was safe. I'm going to start looking for them by systematically going through this room."

The silence was deafening for a moment. Harvey stood up and looked at each of us for a long moment. His eyes rested on me. "We all know someone in this house is involved. I'd say we'd better find out who as fast as possible. We can talk about it in the morning, Jason." He continued looking at me.

I glared at him and wondered if anyone had seriously considered he might possibly be involved. I hadn't until right then. I walked over to the desk to begin my search.

Harvey got ready to leave. "I want it known right now that the specs on microfilm at the office are not going to be touched for any reason. You'd better find the set you have here. You can tell Gramps I'm not going to let anyone touch that microfilm."

I swallowed. No one *told* Gramps much of anything. He did the telling.

Harvey looked at Jason. "You will be into the office in the morning, Jason?" he asked.

Jason nodded. "Yes. In fact, I'll be leaving here soon so I can be at the office early."

Michael started to help me look through the desk in the library when Harvey left. Jason walked Harvey to the door and lingered for some time.

Kyle looked out the window. "You know, there is a slim possibility that J.B. went down to the garage or the stable Sunday morning before I woke. I usually hear him stirring, but I do tend to sleep soundly at times. And he's done it a couple of times before. He could have hidden the specs there, I suppose. On a Sunday morning there's no one around after Barney goes to church." He frowned at the darkness outside. "We'd probably better wait until morning to look. It's doubtful we'd accomplish anything more than to shake up Barney and Tommy at this time of night."

"You have a point there, Kyle," Michael agreed. "One thing's sure. The specs are on the ranch somewhere."

Jason returned, looking at his watch. "I hate to leave you now, but I'd better get home. That blasted rain is really getting started again. I do want to be at the office early in the morning. I have to keep an eye on Harvey. Dad always says Harvey gets a little wild if he's left to his own devices too long. You're bound to find those specs. Let me know when you do." He looked down at me. "Walk me to the door, Laura?"

At the door he took my hands. "As soon as time allows, we'll have to finish the talk we started at the hospital this afternoon."

I was in favor of that. "Yes, we should," I said.

He smiled and said, "Don't take offense at what Harvey said. You know how he is."

"No, I didn't take offense, because I do know Harvey." I lied quite well. I was still angry about it, but it would accomplish nothing to hang on to it.

"Good. I should tell you, Laura, that I'm a little concerned about leaving you here. I don't like these guys involving you in all this. You can leave, you know, even though Gramps says otherwise."

"I know, but I'll stay. I'll be all right."

He dropped a light kiss on my forehead. "I knew you'd say that. It may help me. You can keep me posted on what's going on around here. I'll get out tomorrow as soon as I can. If you become . . . concerned or feel jeopardized by Kyle or Michael, call either Tommy down at the stables or Barney at the garage. I've told them a little of what was going on and asked them to keep an eye on you when they can. You can see I'm worried about you."

Maybe I just wasn't grasping the seriousness of the matter or something, but I couldn't feel any personal danger. I was more angered by everything than intimidated. The fact that the one posing as a kidnapper of Emily was involving me in all this told me something. Since it was obviously an inside job, so to speak, and everyone appeared leery of everyone else in the family, I might well be the logical person for them to want as a go-between. Maybe. What did I know about this sort of thing?

I looked up at Jason's searching eyes. "Thanks for caring."

"Oh, I do care," he said as he took me in his arms. He kissed me lightly.

When he raised his head, I smiled weakly. I was at a loss for words so, as I often do under such circumstances, I took the light way out. "Whew!" I said with my eyes wide.

He smiled down at me. "Hold the thought. I'll be back tomorrow night." He dropped his arms and left.

I closed the front door behind him and turned to face Michael, leaning against the doorjamb of the library. I walked slowly toward him, and his smile broadened as I neared him. "And you said there wasn't anything between you and my little brother!" He was teasing me, and I didn't like it.

"I hardly tell all," I said haughtily and wondered why I said that.

"No woman does." He turned back into the library and took a handful of books from the shelves and felt in back of others.

"And men do?" I asked as I, too, took books from the shelves and started my search.

"Of course. By the way, I don't think our phones have been out tonight. I think Harvey just said that they were as an excuse to come out here. I wish I knew Harvey better. When I was a kid, he always seemed like a disgruntled wimp to me. Gramps has always treated him as though he weren't quite bright."

"I know. I've been a little embarrassed for him at times."

"I know what you mean. Father has treated him

little better. Father told me once that Harvey would worry about the sand on the beach while a tidal wave headed his way. They blow up often."

"Tell me about it. Few employees of Kincade Industries don't have to suffer one of their loud, public disputes from time to time."

"I'm sure it gets pretty hairy sometimes," Michael said. "Another thing, Kyle left and said he'll be back in the morning to help us search the garage and the stables. He didn't say where he was going. It looks like it's just you and me." His smile was mischievous, and his eyes glistened. Did he have to be so handsome?

We had been working systematically through the library shelves for about a half hour when the phone rang. We looked at each other for just a moment before Michael bolted from the room, across the foyer, and into my office to turn on the recorder. When he picked up the phone, I picked up the phone on the library desk.

The man's voice was muffled, but it wasn't a recording. "Tell Miss Grant she should have shown up tonight. It would have been easier on everyone. We wanted to do this without anyone getting hurt while the dingdong is off on one of her trips. Now we're going to have to play rough. We'll really have to grab someone from that family, and you'd better be ready to act. Our time is running short."

"Now see here—" Michael started.

The man cut him off. "Now *you* see here. We'll do this our way. Tell Miss Grant to stay put. If she attempts to leave the ranch, she'll be the first one we pick up. We'll be calling back within twenty-four hours." The phone went dead.

Michael returned to the library and took me in his arms. "Don't you dare make a move without me." He dropped a light kiss on my lips.

"Believe me, you don't have to worry about me going anywhere."

He dropped his arms. "Good. Shall we get back to work?"

We kept at it almost an hour without finding anything; then we decided to call it quits for the night. At my door Michael squeezed my hands as he dropped a light kiss on my nose. "You know I'm going to give my little brother a run for his money. I plan to win."

I slipped my hands out of his grasp. "I don't care to be a trophy either of you wins, thank you." I turned and went into my room. I was so tired I couldn't think of the situation as I got into bed. I hardly remember turning out the light.

When the banging on my door started, my room was still dark. I switched on a light, grabbed a robe, and in my bare feet made it to the door. Michael stood there wearing only his jeans. "Pick up the phone in my room," he said. "I want to turn on the recorder in the office. Our kidnappers are at it again. They say they have Jason now. They want to give you your instructions."

CHAPTER EIGHT

M Y instructions were the same as they had been before. I was to be at Cutter Hill at nine o'clock that night. We weren't given a chance to say anything before the connection was broken. Again it was a recording with a garbled voice. When I hung up, I stepped out into the hall. Michael was bounding up the stairs, and he was furious. "Come on, let's call Jason's apartment and make sure he's not home."

We let the phone ring twenty times. "He's either not home, or he sleeps like the dead," Michael said. "I've got a call to make. Get dressed and meet me in the kitchen. We have to make some plans and find those specs. Something is beginning to seem out of sync here." He looked off over my head as though in thought. "I'd give a lot to know where Kyle is right now."

Emily and Amanda walked out of their rooms at the same time. Amanda, in her usual good humor, asked, "What's going on here? It's the middle of the night, for heaven's sake. Do you two have to wake everyone?"

Emily walked toward us. "I thought I heard a phone a few minutes ago. I always unplug my own phone at night." She wore that confused look I'd grown used to and now knew was a fraud.

Michael told them about the call. Emily frowned and spoke absently. "Why do you suppose they want Laura to bring the specs?"

"They told us before that she was the only one here they trusted."

Amanda made a noise deep in her throat. "That's ridiculous. They're fooling around with our family members. I don't see why they wouldn't trust other family members before they would"—she glanced at Michael, who was watching her steadily—"before they would Laura." I'm sure she had another word she'd have liked to use.

He gave her a patronizing look. "It's assumed it's one of our family members who is involved. That means they know us all, sister dear."

Amanda, totally disgusted with the whole conversation, pulled her robe tighter around her body. "We don't know for sure they have Jason. They said they had Mother when they didn't. Where's Kyle?"

"We'll check on Kyle. Jason doesn't answer his phone. You go back to bed and get your beauty rest."

"We?" Amanda asked with raised eyebrows.

"Laura and I will see what we can do. Whatever it is, we'll be able to do it better if you stay out of our way. We don't need your verbal interference at every turn."

"I don't care for any smart remarks from you. I still think you have something to do with all this."

Michael smiled at his sister. "You're still smarting from the fiasco I saved you from two years ago."

Amanda turned and stomped back into her room.

Emily Kincade sighed dramatically. "Really, Michael, you should be a little gentler with your sister. That was a very embarrassing episode in her life, and you handled it rather bluntly, I'm afraid."

"Bluntly? I had to knock the guy down. I'd never have retrieved those blueprints from his jacket pocket otherwise."

"I suppose," Emily said. "He was quite a handsome young man, though, wasn't he?" She sighed dramatically. "Oh, Michael, do clear up this mess. Jason isn't like you. He needs your help whether he'd like to admit it or not." She waved her hand in the air and turned and walked into her room.

Michael took my elbow and turned me toward my room. "That must have been some character Amanda had trouble with two years ago," I said absently. I was curious, but I didn't want to ask direct questions.

"She didn't have trouble with him; I did. He was an engineer at Kincade Industries. Uncle Harvey and Father thought he was a boy genius with a high degree of curiosity about his work. Father was delighted when he became interested in Amanda. She was too."

I wasn't going to let him stop there. "You weren't crazy about him, I gather."

"I didn't pay any attention to him until I caught him going through the desk in the library one day when everyone was having lunch on the terrace. He said he was looking for a pen. I didn't believe it. I found him the next day in Father's room. He was looking for the bathroom, he said."

"What happened that upset Amanda so?"

He grinned at my curiosity. "Well, I ran a check on him. Under his name of Gary Andover, his record was lily pure. However, I found out about a few industrial espionage cases that were carried out by an inside employee who was an engineer and whose description was surprisingly close to Gary's."

How had he obtained this information? I couldn't stand it any longer. "Michael Kincade, who are you? What are you? What do you do for a living? How could you get that information?"

He pulled me into his arms and dropped his lips to mine. When he raised his head, he lifted his eyebrows high over his dancing eyes. "Now tell me, Laura Grant, just what is life without a little mystery?" His smile was captivating. He stared into my eyes and hypnotized me. Before I could speak, his lips silenced mine, and right then I really didn't mind at all.

When he raised his head, I gasped for air. He grinned down at me, and I had the feeling his eyes were laughing at me. He pulled me close for a moment and surprised me by saying, "I think our chemistry works magic. What do you think?"

The lump in my throat threatened to strangle me.

I gasped for air and eased away from him. "I'm not sure what our chemistry does, but we'd better get moving." I swallowed.

He squeezed my hands. "I'll finish my story over coffee." He turned and left me standing at my door, still breathless.

While I showered and dressed, I wondered why I wasn't more traumatized by Jason's disappearance. Was I numb to the intrigue of the last few days? Nonsense. I was concerned for Jason. I was worried about him. But so many questions ran through my mind, I couldn't sort them out. I thought about Jason and felt a twinge in my chest. I thought of Michael and had a stronger twinge. One thing I had to do was to get my act together, I told myself as I brushed my hair into place.

Michael and Jason were like apples and oranges. It was time I took a good look at reality and tried to find out just where I was going with those two. In the first place, the attention I was receiving from both of them could be nothing more than the manifestation of their sibling rivalry. My back stiffened. I didn't care to be a pawn in that lifelong battle, thank you.

I slammed my brush on the dressing table. Just who did Michael Kincade think he might be! He was an arrogant, superior, insufferable man! I put on my lipstick and then stared at myself in the mirror. "Michael Kincade is stardust in your eyes, Laura Grant. He's worldly, exciting, sophisticated, sure of himself, and breathtakingly handsome. There's a mystique about him. He's so secretive, he drives you crazy. He's also totally out of reach."

I walked over to the window and looked up at the gray sky. I had actually been *talking* to my reflection in the mirror! I couldn't believe I'd done that. I left the room and ran downstairs. Surely it was the hour. A cup of coffee would straighten me out.

Michael was still on the phone in my office when I reached the foyer. I went into the kitchen and silently thanked Mrs. Kiley for having the coffeepot set on a timer to come on at six in the morning. I wondered who Michael was calling. At six forty-five in the morning, there were few people who would be thrilled to hear from him.

I sat down at the table by the bay window and watched the gray sky lighten. I tried to think where J.B. might have hidden those specs. I tried not to think of why, because it aggravated me that he would let everyone think I had hidden them. I didn't for a minute believe anyone had taken them from my hiding place. I glanced at the phone on the wall, and all the lights were out, which meant no one was using the phone. I waited for Michael to join me.

Ten minutes later he walked into the kitchen. He'd combed his hair and put on a shirt and shoes. He poured his coffee and sat down across from me. "Our call came from a pay phone in Sacramento this time. I called Jason's apartment again and didn't get an answer. I let it ring fifteen times." He looked at me and grinned. "I also called the hospital. Father had a quiet night. No change. The nurse said it was good.

We can see him if we want to, but she said they had him heavily sedated and he probably wouldn't respond to us."

"You've been busy." I wondered what other calls he may have made. "I hope it's good news about J.B." I took a sip of my coffee. "I'll continue our search in the library where we left off last night. If we don't find the specs there, do you have any ideas where to look next?"

"Kyle suggested the garage and the stables. It seems a little farfetched to me, but I guess it's worth a try. When we finish the library, every place on this floor will have been checked. Mrs. Kiley went through every corner of this kitchen last night. Marie has checked Gramps's room, against his better judgment. Marie and Mrs. Kiley both checked their rooms even though they were very sure Father hadn't been in them for years.

"Kyle is pretty certain Father wouldn't have gone upstairs. Those blasted things have to be somewhere. It's one of the many times my father may have outsmarted himself. He's done that a few times. It's one of the downfalls of the arrogant, you know."

I had thought about that word *arrogance* in connection with Michael several times. It probably ran in the family. I changed the subject. "Are you going to finish the story about Amanda's boyfriend?"

He studied his cup and looked up at me, smiling. "He stole some blueprints from the library here. Father had brought them home to work on over a long weekend. I saw Gary come out of the library with a bulge in his jacket pocket. I suggested he let me see what caused it, and he refused.

"I accused him of having something he wasn't supposed to have since he wouldn't show whatever it was to me. Of course he denied my statement and was ready to defend his honor with his fists. I connected first, much to the horror of my family.

"However, he did have the blueprints Father had been working on. In his car we found two packed suitcases that held, along with his clothes, copies of many specs and prints from the office files. He planned to leave town when he left the ranch that day. Amanda, of course, was shattered. She has never forgiven me for embarrassing her. There were several guests here that weekend."

Our search of the library proved futile. At eight-thirty I called the office. First I talked to Jason's secretary. Jason had called in and left a message on her answering machine. He told her to cancel all his appointments for a couple of days. He said he'd be unable to come into the office, but he didn't say why. I thought that was curious. Jason was a very methodical and efficient man, but would serious kidnappers let him notify the office that he'd be away?

Next, I talked to Harvey. He already knew about the message on the answering machine, and his fury came through his voice. "I was about to call you out there. He's not there, I gather."

"No." I told him of the phone call we received. Poor Harvey's nerves were on edge. But then, poor

Harvey's nerves were usually on edge. "You'd better find those specs out there, because I'm not authorizing the use of the microfilm. I can't allow it."

"Harvey, you'll have to allow us to make a copy from the microfilm." I tried to stay calm, but I knew Harvey. With both J.B. and Jason away from the office, he was king of the hill, and he was a man who liked being king of the hill. "Jason's life may be at stake."

"Now you just listen here, Miss Grant. I'm in charge here now, and I make the rules. I don't *have* to do *anything*. Our agreement with Watson & Company is that we keep those specs on microfilm and only make the copies that are absolutely necessary for work in progress. That's why I was so against that copy you people had out there in the first place. It shouldn't have been made. But both Father and J.B. were so sure it would be safe. Now look what's happened. You should have taken better care of it. You knew its importance. It could be lost to us, and the whole project could end up down the drain. Those specs could be sold for a fortune. It could cost us a fortune, if someone else gets the jump on us."

When he called me Miss Grant, I knew he was beyond being reasoned with. But if he was agitated, he had me right up there with him. "Now, Harvey, I'll talk to Gramps if I have to. Tell Ted Granger not to leave the office. We may need him."

"Ted Granger has a dentist appointment this morning. I'm not sure when he'll be back."

I clamped my teeth. I'd find out who his dentist

was and when he'd be back. Harvey's tone of voice told me it was useless to talk to him further on the phone. "I'll talk to you later, Harvey." I hung up.

Michael had been listening in. He hadn't wanted to speak to Harvey himself. "I always set that old boy off. You can handle him better," he assured me. I doubted anyone could handle Harvey for long.

"Is Granger the one you said is the only one who can open that safe?" Michael asked me.

"Yes. Jerry Vacaro is on vacation, and J.B., of course, is unavailable. Those three are the only ones with the combination."

"Great," Michael said without enthusiasm.

We got on with our search of the garage and the stable and they, too, proved fruitless. Down at the stable, Tommy Allen did mention something interesting. He said that Jason was the only family member he'd seen on Sunday, and he was sure J.B. hadn't been down at the stables since his first stroke.

He grinned at me as he told Michael that Jason had come down to use the phone. "He said he'd just as soon Laura didn't hear him breaking a date. He'd decided not to go into Sacramento until Monday morning. Of course, when J.B. had his stroke Sunday night, that changed his plans. I didn't see anyone from the house on Monday.

"Jason came down last night again, before he left for Sacramento, and made another call. He complained about how hard it always was to make a private phone call at the house. He reminded me of you boys years ago. You always complained about no privacy. He used the private line I have in my quarters, just like you boys used to do when you were home from college." He laughed.

For a minute Michael looked off at the horses frolicking in the sun in the big corral. Then he broke into a grin. He looked back at the gray-haired man. "Tommy, I, too, would like to use your phone one more time."

Tommy regaled me with a story about Michael learning to break a horse, while Michael made his call. Michael's call took so long, I was ready to check on him when he joined us. He took my arm and aimed me toward the house. "We're going to Sacramento," he said.

We returned to the house and changed our clothes. I wasn't about to wear jeans to the office. I met Michael in the foyer. He, too, had changed out of his jeans. I laid my shoulder bag on the table and said what was on my mind. "Before we go any further, I'd like to have my say."

He looked surprised. "Okay, go ahead."

I cleared my throat. "I know your father didn't want the sheriff brought in on this, because he feels it's a family affair. I just don't happen to agree with him at this point. I think we should call in the sheriff. If Jason is in danger—"

He put up his hand to stop me. "Okay, Laura, I'll tell you this much. The sheriff is fully informed, just as he was when we thought someone had kidnapped Mother. It was the FBI that put the tap on our phones. Everyone knows how Father feels, and they're willing to keep a low profile as long as it's not counterproductive." He smiled at my shocked expression. "That's why I've spent so much time on the phone. When we got that first call about Mother, I took matters into my own hands."

"I see." A lot of things fell into place, almost. I held my head to one side. "I know I asked this earlier this morning, but I have to ask again. Michael Kincade, who are you?"

He grinned and took my arm. "You'll know soon. When this is all over, I think you and I will be ready for a long, long talk. I promise to tell you all. I'm sure that if our chemistry was in the lab, there'd be an explosion. I really think we should do something about it, and I'm not going to want to hear anything about the time element. You'll also know why I feel I met you at the perfect time in my life. Maybe there is such a thing as fate or destiny connected with love."

He surprised me by dropping a fleeting kiss on my forehead. I felt everything about Michael was fleeting. I wanted to dissect his statement, especially his use of the word love, but he grabbed my arm.

"Come," he said as he aimed me at the front door, "it's time we invaded Kincade Industries and shook up Uncle Harvey. You might like to know Jason used Tommy's phone last night to call Uncle Harvey on Harvey's car phone."

We both opted to sidestep the present on the ride into town. He talked of the changes he'd seen when he drove through Sacramento. I talked about my adjustment to Sacramento and how much I loved the same could be said about me and a few others who lived at the house.

Harvey didn't act thrilled to see us. After a self-righteous defense of his refusal to allow us to make a copy of the specs from microfilm, Harvey finally gave in when I picked up the phone to call the ranch, wake Gramps from his morning nap, and tell him of our predicament.

Ted Granger had not returned from the dentist. His secretary called the dentist's office and was told Ted would be back within the hour. Just as we turned to leave Harvey, Michael asked the question I'd been waiting for him to ask. "Tell me, Uncle Harvey, why did Jason call you on your car phone after you left the ranch last night?"

Harvey's mouth fell open, and his eyes flashed between Michael and me. "I didn't hear from Jason. . . ." His words came slowly.

I jumped in. "Harvey, we know Jason called you last night. He called you from Tommy's phone at the stable. We had the call traced. You've been asked a simple question and, under the circumstances, I would say it's to everyone's best interest, especially Jason's, if you tell us just what he said."

Small beads of perspiration blossomed on his forehead. He adjusted his glasses and cleared his throat. "Jason wanted to know"—he cleared his throat again—"what time I'd be in this morning. We have that Kimball matter to discuss. He wanted to settle it right away this morning. You know how Jason is, Laura—he likes to get at things early."

mountains. We both worked to keep our conv
in neutral.

And then we fell silent as we neared Sacran.
My mind went off on its own. He, too, said we'd
a chat when this was all over. Who would do it fir
Jason or Michael? I just might tell them both to t.
a hike, I thought. I knew I was lying to myself, b
it made me feel better for at least a minute.

I looked out at the sun glistening on the American
River as we neared the center city. After three days
of on-again and off-again rain, the sun was welcome.
I was infuriated with Michael for being so mysteri-
ous, but I realized I couldn't afford to spend any time
or effort on it just then. There were more serious matters at hand.

We had called Jason's apartment several times during the morning, and it proved to be a fruitless endeavor. I hoped Harvey's mood had improved since
I talked to him earlier, but going by past experience,
I knew it wasn't likely. I envisioned him stomping
around the offices and labs with all the humility of
Napoleon.

The office was full of whispers when we walked in.
I suspected Michael was the subject most under discussion as we walked through the reception area and
the general accounting offices. I nodded to Ralph Satterly, who was smiling as usual. He wasn't above suspicion yet in my books, but I really didn't have a single thing to tie him into anything. He'd been at the
house when the explosion occurred, and he'd come
in after we received the call about Emily. But the

I narrowed my eyes at Harvey. "It doesn't wash, Harvey. Everyone at Kincade Industries knows that you come through that front door on the dot of eight o'clock every morning. Everyone is judged early or late depending if they arrive before or after you do. You're more dependable than the clocks around here." I wondered if I was talking myself out of a job, but it was not my immediate concern. This fat little bald man was lying through his teeth.

He took out his handkerchief and wiped the perspiration from his brow. "Okay, okay. He wanted me to call some woman and apologize to her for him. I guess he stood her up. He has a lot of girls, you know, Laura, in case you thought you had a monopoly on him by living at the house." There was a sneer in his voice, and if I'd been a man. . . .

Michael jumped in. "Okay, Uncle Harvey, back off." He looked at me, and I was frowning. I shook my head. I hadn't believed that story, either, but not for any reason Harvey might conjure up. Michael got my point. "Look, Harvey"—he dispensed with the Uncle—"if anything happens to Jason because of your conniving little ego, you be ready to answer to me."

Michael took my arm, and we left Kincade Industries, saying we would be back within the hour. I could feel Harvey's eyes burning into my back. We stopped and impressed on Ted Granger's secretary how important it was for us to see him. I wasn't sure Harvey would do that.

Outside, I let out a long breath. Michael laughed.

"You sure do know how to get to Uncle Harvey and make him sweat. Poor Harvey, he sees himself as a victim of the world."

"He's a victim of himself."

"Most of us are."

"Michael," I began, frowning up at the sun, "I'd like to go to Jason's apartment."

We turned toward the parking lot. "Something's bugging you, isn't it?" he asked.

I nodded. "Yes, but I don't know what it is."

"Is it something you learned or a feeling you have?"

"Neither. It's more like the hair on the back of my neck."

He hurried me along. "That's good enough for me, anytime."

CHAPTER NINE

No one answered our knock at Jason's apartment. The luxury apartment building was deadly quiet. Michael started fooling with the lock. "What are you doing?" I asked, not wanting to believe what I was watching.

"Never mind. Just turn around and let me know if you see anyone coming in our direction."

"You're picking the lock!"

"Yeah."

"Is that your profession, the one you don't want to tell anyone about?" My eyes darted back and forth, up and down the hall. My heart raced, and my palms became damp.

"Not full-time," he answered glibly.

I know when I'm being laughed at, but I didn't think this was a laughing matter. "What if we get caught?" I asked.

"Plead either insomnia or insanity."

"I'll go for insanity. It'll be more believable. Do hurry, if you must do this."

"You don't happen to have a key, do you?"

"No." I kept my eyes glued to the hallway.

"The more expensive the apartment, the more expensive the locks, you know. Something has to be done to justify the exorbitant amount of money it takes to live in one of these places."

"I guess you know about that sort of thing."

"Ummm," he mumbled, and it was just a moment later when he said, "Ah!" and pushed the door open.

I leaped inside, breathing heavily. "For heaven's sake, close the door!" I had the feeling everyone in the building had seen us.

Michael smiled and looked around. "You know your way around this apartment, do you?"

I frowned. "No, I do not. I'm not even sure why I wanted to come here or what to look for, but maybe we'll find something. I'm going to look around."

Michael went into an alcove that held a desk and two chairs. I looked around the kitchen, dining room, living room, and the guest room and bath. As I would have expected, Jason had good taste. It was decorated in a contemporary decor that touched on elegance. I started into the master bedroom, and Michael called to me. "Laura, does Jason go to New York often?"

"Not that I know about. I know he hasn't gone there since I've been working at Kincade Industries, unless he did it on a weekend or while I was on vacation. Why do you ask?"

"His phone book has a lot of numbers with the area code of 212. That's New York City. Some are listed under first names only, and some are under first and last names. Odd, huh?"

"Odd, indeed," I answered. "Even Kincade Industries has little to do with New York. Just about everybody we do business with is west of the Mississippi." It occurred to me to tell Michael about Jason's gambling, but I thought better of it. Michael wasn't one hundred percent in the clear with me yet. Maybe ninety-nine percent, but not one hundred.

I left and wandered into Jason's bedroom. The bed was neatly made, and I could smell, just faintly, the scent of after-shave lotion. I stuck my head in the bathroom, and the scent was much stronger. I looked back into the bedroom and noticed three coat hangers lying on the bed. The door to the walk-in closet was ajar, so I opened it. On the floor three suitcases sat lined up to one side. Between the smallest one and the next one was a space just about the size another suitcase might have called home.

"Michael, come in here."

Michael strolled in. "You called?"

I pointed to the suitcases and the hangers on the bed.

Michael looked around and nodded. "Either brother Jason packed to go away for a while, or someone packed for him. How interesting. You're quite a detective."

"Take a deep breath," I said.

"It smells like after-shave to me."

"It does to me too. Come into the bathroom." He sniffed around the bathroom and looked around. I went on. "After-shave lingers a while after a man shaves, but not a long while. Either Jason has been here recently and shaved, or someone else was here, packed for him, and shaved while he was at it." I opened the medicine cabinet and the cabinet under the sink. "There's no razor of any type here that I can see, nor is there a bottle of after-shave. I'm not sure what all this tells us."

"I'm not, either, but I'm going to have these New York phone numbers checked. We may find out my little brother has a secret life."

I made a face. "It seems to run in the family. Your mother had one, you live one, and Jason thinks Kyle has one. What a family!"

"And just think—you're destined to be part of it." He turned and walked out of the room telling me, "Come, we've got things to do."

After Harvey reluctantly allowed me to make a copy of the specs for Hardcase, Michael and I stopped at Jason's office. Michael talked to Jason's secretary, while I went into his office and looked through his phone book. There was only one New York number in it. I copied it down. The rest of the phone book contained listings of firms' names I recognized or people I knew.

On our way to the parking lot, Michael told me what he'd found out. "According to Jason's secretary, Jason has done no traveling for Kincade Industries in all the time he's been there. I'd say her tenure is a lot longer than his. J.B. and Harvey traveled a little, but not Jason."

"It's said she was hired by the first Kincade who started Kincade Industries. That would be Gramps's grandfather, you know."

I handed him the phone number I had copied. "If this isn't one of the numbers Jason has in the phone book at his apartment, you might check it out too."

Michael pulled out the list he had copied down at the apartment. "Nope," he said, "this is a new one."

I scowled as he opened the door of his car. "Have we done something illegal by copying those phone numbers?"

He laughed at me. "Don't worry about it. Wait here a minute. I'm going to call these numbers in to a friend of mine. He might have something for us by the time we reach the ranch. Also, think about where we might have lunch. I'm starved."

Thinking of a restaurant was no problem, but it occurred to me that neither Michael nor I had mentioned our trip to Jason's apartment to Harvey. I didn't know if Michael had a reason, but I couldn't think what mine might be except that I didn't care to tell Harvey anything.

Seated in an uncrowded restaurant, surrounded by more hanging ferns than anyone needs with lunch, and our orders given, Michael reached over and picked up my hand. "Laura, I know there are a lot of things bothering you. I wish you'd decide you can trust me. Believe me, I *am* one of the good guys. I wouldn't have brought the sheriff and the FBI in on this if I was hiding something, would I?"

I looked into his eyes and had to look away. They had a way of marring my judgment, but he was right. The FBI does more than sit idly around waiting for our phone to ring. The chances were good we'd all been checked out. Of course, I didn't know for sure the FBI had been brought in. I had only his word. I looked back at him. I had to trust someone, and I decided to trust my instincts. They told me Michael really was one of the good guys, as he insisted.

I squeezed his hand and nodded. "You're right— a lot of things are bothering me. I feel a little . . . dumb about some of them, but they stay right with me."

"Tell me anyway. You're too beautiful to be dumb."

I took a deep breath. "Okay, you're going to get it all, but don't forget, you asked for it."

He smiled and said, "Okay, I'll remember. Go."

"First of all, Jason can have friends in New York that you and I wouldn't know about, but that scent of after-shave says loud and clear that someone shaved in that apartment just minutes before we arrived. That scent doesn't last a long time. Also, although I usually hate to *assume* anything, I think there is evidence enough for us to reasonably assume some of his clothes and a suitcase are missing.

"We received that call telling us that Jason had been abducted about six this morning. Things just don't fit. Why would he or anyone else be at his apartment at eleven or eleven-thirty this morning to pick up his things? And shave? Also"—I hesitated just a moment, hating the things I was thinking about Jason—"do you know Jason does quite a bit of gambling?"

Michael looked at his coffee for a minute. "He used to do it quite recklessly in college, but I'd thought he'd outgrown it. He borrowed money from me a few times, and I think Kyle bailed him out a time or two also. He got in trouble with it only once to my knowledge. He really got in over his head, and he was out of his league. I couldn't come up with enough money at the time to bail him out, and when he got roughed up one night, I went to Father. Father bailed him out, but I don't think Jason ever forgave me. He said he'd never trust me again." He shrugged. "It was his problem. Do you know much about his gambling these days?"

Now I knew why Jason had told me not to trust Michael. Feeling a little guilty and disloyal, I told Michael what little I knew about Jason's gambling. Michael became thoughtful again, but he didn't comment. "Also," I went on, "did you know that he and Harvey had a long talk the night of the explosion after we all went to bed?"

"I heard him telling you that the next morning."

"Well, Jason was acting very strange that morning. His attitude toward me was very odd too. It was like he was a different person, even more businesslike than he is at the office, more brusque, and it was as though I were someone he'd just met. It didn't last.

He was his old self later in the day. I've never figured out his real reason for wanting to close the office at the ranch. I don't profess to know what it all means, but it's bothered me."

He nodded. "Strange, huh?" was his only comment.

I forged ahead. "Also, Amanda asked me about the Hardcase project shortly after I moved into the house. To my knowledge, at that time, it was the world's best-kept secret. I've wondered why she didn't mention she knew about it the night of the explosion. I can't imagine your father told her about it. They hardly ever say a civil word to each other—at least, when I'm around."

"Now that is interesting. It's true—she and Father have always locked horns. Remember, I told you I saw her talking to Kyle after you took that envelope upstairs." He grinned. "The plot thickens."

Our lunch arrived, but once started, I couldn't stop. I wanted to get it all out. "I don't want you to think I'm paranoid about your family, but—"

He interrupted me. "It's all right if you are. Paranoia comes easy, once you get to know everyone."

"Your father talks almost daily with someone on the phone. He wants the door to my office closed, he talks in a hushed voice, and he's generally in a foul mood after he hangs up."

"And the plot thickens and thickens," he said, grinning broadly.

His reaction annoyed me, but I was determined to air out the things that were bugging me. "Because these people, whoever they are, are involving me in all this, there are things I'd like to know about your family."

"Ask away. I've been away a lot, so I don't know all, but you're welcome to what I do know."

"Okay. First, I have the feeling Gramps is a little suspicious of your mother. It's hard for me to believe, and I've wondered why."

"Well, I love the old boy, but Gramps has his quirks, as you know. The way I heard it, Gramps had Father's future wife picked out for him. Good family, old friend's daughter, and all that jazz, but Father married Mother and told Gramps afterward. Gramps is one who, at times, doesn't get mad, he gets even. He's been on Mother's case all her married life. She ignores him, thankfully. Her disappearing acts used to send him into a rage, when he noticed, but it got him nowhere. When she returned, she'd smile and walk away while he carried on. It's always annoyed me that Father didn't go to her defense. I've never seen him do it." He took a vicious bite from his sandwich.

I'd touched a nerve, but that cleared that up. "Okay, what about the tenuous relationship Harvey has with your father and Gramps? They both seem to be on his case all the time."

That brought a smile to Michael's eyes. "You know Uncle Harvey. I guess he's got it in certain areas, but it sends pure terror through both Father and Gramps if they think he's done something for Kincade Industries totally on his own. His judgment leaves something to be desired, to say the least. I've heard about a couple of boners he pulled. Gramps treats him as though he's a not-too-bright ten-year-old, and Father treats him as though he's a necessary nuisance most of the time. I've never been sure why Uncle Harvey takes it." He shrugged. "I guess family ties bind tight for some."

"Not you, though." A smile forced itself on my lips.

"Nope. Anything else?"

I thought for a minute while I took a bite of my sandwich. "Well, I've done a lot of wondering about Kyle. I caught him a few times looking at papers on my desk. I don't know what it means, but it bothers me. I heard he spends some time at his father's house, then he moves in with your father, and then he drops out of sight for a while. I'll admit, I've given Kyle a wide berth and don't know him very well at all even though we've lived in the same house for over a month. He seems harmless enough. I know he spends an enormous amount of time on the phone."

"Kyle has always been addicted to the telephone. I used to tease him a lot, but he always said it saves gas. He likes to keep in touch with his friends, I guess, but he's not too interested in spending much time with them. It's easier to control the time and conversation on the phone.

"Nobody knows Kyle well except maybe Mother. I think, at times, she was closer to Kyle than she was to Amanda, Jason, or me. They have some kind of a bond. Kyle and Amanda have always been pretty good friends too. His mother, my father's sister, died when Kyle was pretty young, and his father, Uncle Teddy, never remarried. Kyle kind of grew up with us. Uncle Teddy is lost somewhere in the banking system, but he's done all right. Never hear much about him, these days, now that I think of it."

"I've never heard of him at all," I said. We stood up to leave the restaurant, being careful not to bang our heads on the hanging pots of fern. "Have you and Kyle always gotten along all right?" I asked. In that family, it was easy to lose track.

"I've never had any problems with Kyle, but we've never been close, either. He's always gone his way, and I've gone mine. It burns everyone that he doesn't work. However, I've heard he doesn't ask anyone for money, either. It's very curious, but it's certainly none of my business. It has occurred to me that possibly Mother subsidizes him." He shrugged. "That's hardly any of my business, either."

I shook my head. "Your family could drive a sane person over the edge."

"I know," he said flatly.

We were almost to the ranch when one more thing that had been bothering me flashed into my mind. "Michael, why do you think we get our calls so early in the morning and the drop time for the specs is either at dawn or in the evening? We haven't heard from them once during the day."

"I've thought about that. It usually indicates that someone has a job during the day and can't make phone calls. It could be that someone doesn't want to be missed during the day. No matter who may be involved from inside the family household, I'd guess that someone from Kincade Industries is also involved."

"I've thought of that too. With the calls coming in to us and Jason missing, and the ransom demanded, anyone in the firm could be suspect. I stepped into personnel while you were romancing Jason's secretary and asked a friend of mine to get me a list of anyone who missed work yesterday and today and their reasons. He'll call this afternoon. It could prove interesting."

"You're being a good detective again. I asked for the same thing from Jason's secretary. She said she'd call me this afternoon too."

I thought of Jason's silver-haired secretary. "You must have really turned on your charm. It's said she guards company information like a bulldog."

He shrugged. "I do what I can, Miss Grant. I do what I can."

He flashed his smile at me, and as usual my smile broadened. I sobered quickly. It was almost four o'clock, and we still had things to do. I couldn't have named them, but I was sure we had a lot of things to do.

The large brown envelope I had clutched in my hand reminded me that Jason was missing—and I had a rendezvous with his kidnapper. . . .

*   *   *

When we entered the house, Mrs. Kiley met us at the door. "Laura, there's a call for you on line four, and Gramps wants to see you both right away."

I looked up at Michael. "You go ahead to Gramps's rooms. I'll take my call and meet you there." If it was my mother, asking me about life on a real horse ranch, as she did every single week, I'd scream. When I answered the phone, a man's well-modulated voice spoke to me.

"Miss Grant, so glad I caught you. I'm leaving town for an indefinite time, and I want to get a message to J.B. So sorry to hear about his second stroke. He told me to leave a message with you and no one else, if he couldn't be reached. I'm afraid you'll have to tell him the Cauldfield deal is down the drain. He'll know what I mean."

I had absolutely no idea who was speaking. "Sir, who are you?"

"Oh, yes. I'm Terrance Pearson. J.B. and I made a sizable investment in what was to be a very large shopping mall here in Sacramento. We've been talking daily for some time since we found out there might be trouble."

"Trouble?" I asked.

"Well, yes. It seems now that rather than some funds being lost in the bookkeeping system as we were told, one of the general partners has secretly departed and has, apparently, hidden himself and the money quite successfully."

"In other words, he's taken the money and vanished without a trace."

"Quite."

"I'm gathering it's a large sum of money."

"Yes indeed, and unfortunately J.B. and I used to have possession of quite a large portion of that money. I'm afraid we both invested quite an inappropriate amount of money in this venture. It did seem to be quite solid, with very respectable people involved. I'm afraid J.B.'s father was adamantly against this endeavor.

"I believe the old man has usually kept a tight fist on any and all investments made for the family. J.B. has done only careful investing on his own that involved comparatively small amounts of money. This time, without telling his father, J.B. took a substantial loan against the ranch to make the size of investment he wanted to. When the funds more or less disappeared, J.B. became quite agitated."

"I'm sure." I was more than sure. I waited, feeling the man wasn't through talking.

"I'm telling you this, Miss Grant, because J.B. assured me you would be the soul of discretion in the matter and I could tell you anything that might be pertinent. I feel, with him in the hospital, you should be aware of the whole situation as it exists. I did want you to realize that this is not a generally known venture in the family circle there, and I'm sure J.B. wants it kept that way. He'll find some delicate way to break it to his father when he recovers, I hope."

Marvelous. Now I knew what J.B.'s phone calls were about and why he was cranky when he hung up. I'd wait until long after he recovered before I told him that juicy morsel. Unless, of course, he asked. I hoped I wouldn't be around when Gramps found out.

Gramps was in a grouchy mood. "I want to know what in thunder is going on! Where have you two been, and what are you doing to help matters?"

Michael, with more patience than I felt I had at the moment, explained all to Gramps. When he heard about the problems we had with Harvey, which Michael explained in more detail than I probably would have managed, Gramps exploded. "If he were an employee, I'd have bounced him years ago!"

Michael raised an eyebrow. "You've been saying that for a long time, Gramps. Maybe some of Kincade Industries' problems through the generations are that it has been run too much on blood." He went on and finished the story of our day.

Gramps listened intently and was thoughtful for a minute after Michael finished. He hit the arm of his wheelchair. "Michael, I certainly hope you can unravel this mess as easily as you took care of that guy a couple of years ago! I've never figured out why there are always so many blackguards in our family." He picked up the empty pipe he often carried in his mouth and studied it. "You're probably right. Too much nepotism. Too much adherence to the bloodline. What you need for a business can't be bred." Marie came in with his medication. He looked up at Michael. "Throw this woman out. I fired her an hour ago, and she's still here."

Marie grimaced. "You've been firing me every other day for years, but I'm still here. I'm just a glutton for punishment. Now take your medicine, and then you *will* take a nap, if I have to use a needle to make you do it." She looked at us and winked.

We promised to keep Gramps advised and left.

Mrs. Kiley met us again. "Michael, you have a call, and your mother wants to see you and Laura in her rooms as soon as you're free."

We looked at each other and took a deep breath. "If we weren't so popular, we might be able to get something done," Michael said as we mounted the stairs. "Come, I'll take the call in my room. It might be about the phone numbers."

CHAPTER TEN

MICHAEL wrote swiftly as he listened to his caller. He handed me the list, but he continued to listen. Finally he spoke. "Thanks, Franklin. If I'm not here when you call back, leave your name, and I'll call you when we get home." He listened again and then said, "Yeah, the drop is at nine." He hung up. I was still studying the list. "Know any of those firms?" he asked.

"I'm not sure. Somewhere I've heard of Stone Industries, Matheson, Inc., and Gilroy & Son, Inc., but I'm not sure where. Maybe it will come to me. I never heard of the others."

"Franklin will check them all out and let us know what kind of businesses they are. Maybe that will tell us something. If we need it, he'll find out what contact Jason has had with them."

The age-old question came to mind: *Michael Kincade, who are you?* This time I didn't ask it, but it haunted me. How could he obtain all this information? This wasn't stuff just any person could call up and get. I put the list into my pocket, and we went to his mother's room.

Emily had a suite of rooms. The large sitting room was a maze of various shades of lilac and gray and off-white. It was a fluffy room, just like the image she so well portrayed. There was a small room to the right, with a tablelike desk and a chair. A wicker basket, with a mattress, sat beside the desk for Daisy, who greeted Michael and me with great enthusiasm.

Emily's bedroom was off to the left. It was a large room, with white furniture trimmed with gilt. That room, too, had an abundance of lilac and gray. The whole suite looked very much like Emily Kincade herself. Two large packages, wrapped in brown paper, sat in the corner of the sitting room. She greeted us and spoke to Daisy. "Go get Amanda, dear."

I couldn't help smiling as the small dog ran out the door, crossed the hall to Amanda's room, and barked softly. Amanda opened the door and disappeared for a minute before she entered Emily's room with Kyle and Daisy behind her.

Emily smiled and said, "It's so nice to have you all here. I'm sorry Jason can't be with us, but I hope he'll be back with us shortly." She waved her hand in the air. "Do sit down, children."

We all did as we were told. I don't know about anyone else, but I had to tell myself there was no need to hold my breath.

Kyle spoke before Emily could go on. "Anything new on Jason, Michael?"

"Afraid not," Michael replied.

Emily smiled again. "First, I must tell you, I just finished talking with Dr. Stuart. J.B. is doing nicely. His vital signs are excellent. By tomorrow they hope to take him off the strong medication he is on now, and by late in the day, or Thursday morning, we may be able to see him and talk to him."

We all acknowledged the good news. I don't know what I expected, but again I had to tell myself not to hold my breath. She went on, talking more like the confused, vague woman I'd first met than the successful writer who had talked to us the night before. I decided that possibly that role was more comfortable for her with her family.

She talked about her confession of the night before and how difficult it had been to keep it all a secret and then to admit it. I shifted in my chair. Her monologue seemed to go on endlessly, and it was a little like waiting for the other shoe to drop. And then she looked at Kyle and smiled. "It's Kyle's turn now. We've decided that, under the circumstances, it's time for him to reveal his secret life also. The floor is yours, Kyle."

Amanda, Michael, and I looked at each other. Our puzzlement showed clearly on our faces. With J.B. in the hospital and Jason held by kidnappers, it was apparently time to tell all for some of the Kincade clan! Who was next? Michael maybe? Not likely. I wondered what Kyle had been hiding.

Kyle stood up and brought the brown paper-wrapped packages over to his chair. He ran his hand through his straight brown hair and grinned sheepishly. "Somehow I feel I'm back in elementary school, about to tell the class what I did on my summer vacation." We all laughed. "Contrary to public opinion," he began, "I've not been quite the shiftless oaf I'm thought to be. Because Emily has bared her soul to you all and because I'm having a private show in Sacramento this next weekend and there is going to be a spread about it in tomorrow's paper, along with an interview and picture of me, I decided I'd better tell all also." He hesitated and grinned, and his embarrassment showed. He did feel like a kid in school. It surprised me. I wouldn't have expected him to feel uneasy being or doing anything.

Amanda frowned, and her usual impatience came through. "Get on with it, Kyle. What kind of a show are you having, for heaven's sake?"

He unwrapped one of the packages and revealed an oil painting of the ranch at sunset. I gasped. It was absolutely beautiful. The detail brought every tree, all the white fences, and the horses cavorting in the corral to life. I couldn't believe the texture, the color, the beauty. "Kyle, this is magnificent!" I was stumped for words. In the corner of the painting was the name Kyle Marklin.

Amanda, for once, was at a loss for words too. "Kyle, it's great. I . . . can't believe it. Why didn't you tell me?" There was anger in her voice.

He shrugged and looked at Michael. I was surprised by Michael's knowledge of art. He commented on the composition, the colors, and the strokes in terms I barely understood. He clapped Kyle on the back. "You shouldn't have kept this a secret, Kyle. You do noteworthy work."

"Thanks, Michael. I've done fairly well in San Francisco and L.A. I never could bring myself to tell either my father or yours. I just always had an image of what would happen if they found out I was an artist. It used to upset them, if you'll remember, that I was never too interested in football. You and Jason did so well, they just took for granted I should too." He laughed.

"Well, you did keep the bench warm a couple of seasons," Michael replied, still looking at the painting with admiration.

"Yeah, and that was it. After graduation, when I refused positions at both Kincade Industries and the bank, I felt they'd appreciate me more as a ne'er-do-well but someone they could call on in emergencies than they would as an artist."

Emily smiled her vague smile. "I did agree with Kyle on that point. None of the Kincade men of my generation understand much beyond commerce of some sort."

Kyle went on. "Aunt Em not only understood but subsidized me that first year. After that I started paying my own way. I've been fortunate to be able to make a living with it since then. I've done a lot of very profitable commissions." He glanced at Emily, who beamed with pride.

"Where do you do your work, Kyle?" I asked.

"Uncle Harvey lets me use his guest house. He's

known for some time, and he's kept my secret although he has no appreciation for what I do."

The information surprised me. Harvey couldn't be all bad. Michael looked at his watch and stood up. "Kyle, I hope we'll be able to make your show." He slipped his arm around my waist, rather possessively, I thought, and added, "Laura and I have to go. We have a few things to do before we make the drop tonight."

"I'll expect you both at my show, now that you're officially invited. I'll leave the information on Laura's desk. You didn't find the specs here, I gather. I talked to Tommy and Barney when I arrived, and they said you and Laura had scoured the stables and the garage to no avail."

"We got a copy from the reluctant Harvey at the office. Look, we'll see you later." Michael turned me to the door.

I squeezed Kyle's hand, seeing him in a completely new light. I stopped in the hall and stepped back into Emily's room. There were things I had to know. "Kyle, I'm asking everyone this. Where were you last night and this morning?"

He gave me a puzzled look for a minute before he answered. "I didn't mention it, with all that's been going on around here, but my father's been quite ill. Last night his housekeeper called me just before Aunt Em came home and told me Dad was having another ulcer attack. When I left here, I went over there and stayed up with her and Dad until after five this morning. The sun was almost all the way up before I fell asleep in a chair. She woke me about ten this morning. That's why I didn't get here earlier today."

I said, "Oh." It would be easy enough to check, but I believed him. I thought of something else. "I caught you looking at the papers on my desk a few times after I first moved here. Were you looking for anything in particular?"

He grinned. "Nope. I was just fascinated with all those printouts you had. The world of computers is more strange to me than life on Mars." He laughed lightly. "Really, Laura, there was no ulterior motive to my curiosity. I've just never seen much of that stuff, and I had no idea what I was looking at."

I believed him. Unless he was an accomplished actor, I doubted he could look more baffled by my question. I hesitated before I asked the big question of Amanda. "Amanda, would you mind telling me how you knew about the Hardcase project? You asked me about it almost as soon as I arrived."

She gave me her bored look. "Are you assuming the role of our in-house D.A., Laura?" She looked over at Michael and quickly looked back at me. "I'd heard Gramps and Father talking about it. They acted as if it were the Holy Grail, for heaven's sake. When I asked Father what the Hardcase project was, he nearly bit my head off. My curiosity was aroused." Her expression changed, and she grinned at Kyle. "After the explosion I knew Hardcase was something really important. I got even more curious. I told Kyle to let me know if he heard anything about it."

Kyle picked up the tale. "When J.B. gave you that

envelope, I thought it had the specs. I told Amanda later that he'd given it to you. When your room was ransacked, it occurred to me for a minute that either Amanda or her wimp of a boyfriend, Ralph, might have done it. I felt guilty for telling her until I remembered they'd been out playing tennis until it started to rain. I'm not sure when they came in, but I doubt it was too long before Mrs. Kiley called me to help straighten your room."

"Thanks a lot, Kyle, for your vote of confidence," Amanda said with sarcasm in her voice. "We were only inside about ten or fifteen minutes before Ralph came to get me."

I looked at Amanda as though I liked her. It wouldn't have taken too long to trash my room that way. "It surprised me that you had asked me about Hardcase, but you didn't mention that you knew about it the night of the explosion."

She looked bored again. "All I knew was the name. I had no idea what you all were talking about, and I still don't. I knew no one would tell me. I didn't have anything to say except that I'd heard the name."

Slowly but surely I was losing all my suspects. I didn't doubt either Amanda or Kyle.

When I stepped back into the hall, Michael was waiting. "Do you have any suspects left?" he asked.

"I think it's getting down to you or me," I said dryly.

"My thoughts exactly."

Mrs. Kiley met us at the bottom of the stairs. "I'm beginning to feel like a secretary. I have messages for both of you and, do you know, they're the same." She handed us each a piece of paper, but she looked up at Michael. "Your mother told me she didn't want to be disturbed while she had you in her rooms."

My list was from the personnel department at Kincade Industries. The day before, there were three people who didn't show up. One woman had been out three days last week with the flu and was still fighting it. One of the lab men couldn't make it in because his wife had a baby at four that morning. The third absentee was a janitor who had been in an auto accident Sunday and was in the hospital. That day Janet Bailey from personnel was out because her child came down with the measles. The woman with the flu was still out, as well as the man in the hospital. The new father was back at work. The report was no help. Michael's report was from Jason's secretary and, of course, said the exact same thing.

Those company names were still rattling around in my head. I knew I'd heard them before, but I couldn't think where. Michael and I sat down in the library with a cup of coffee and rehashed everything we knew and the things we wished we knew. We couldn't get away from the fact that someone connected to this household had to be involved. The fact that the dogs let them break in Saturday night verified it, if nothing else.

"You know, Michael," I said, staring at a row of books, "whoever these kidnappers might be, obviously they just took advantage of the fact that Emily disappeared Sunday. Knowing she was usually gone for four or five days at a time, they felt safe saying they held her hostage in their call Sunday. They knew no one could deny it. However, they had no way of knowing she would cut her trip down to two days that one time. That must have rattled their cage."

"I bet," he said. I wasn't sure how much attention he paid to what I said. He, too, was staring at a line of books, nearly oblivious to me.

I'd kept the envelope containing the specs in my hand or beside me in a chair since Harvey gave it to me. I think it amused Michael.

I was about to comment on the subject when Kyle joined us. He slouched into a chair and looked over at me. "Laura, since I heard about Jason's abduction today, I've been thinking. It's asking one heck of a lot to expect you to take that trip out to Cutter Hill alone. It will be dark, and you'll be very vulnerable. I'll gladly take your place."

My antennae went up. Was he willing because he was concerned about me, or did it appear an easy way to get the specs?

Michael saved me from answering. "Both times they have insisted Laura bring the specs. They've said they'll be watching her. Now, usually this type of person means what they say, and it's not a good idea to try to con them. They have said if she doesn't do the delivering, the deal is off. They claim she's the only one they'll trust not to try to pull something. I don't like it, either, Kyle, and I'll do what I can."

"You sound like you know what you're talking about, Michael." He raised his eyebrows. "Some might say you sound experienced on one side or the other." He grinned, but Michael didn't comment. "You know we should have notified the authorities as soon as that safe was blown," Kyle went on. "I don't think we should have given J.B. his way."

I glanced at Michael, who apparently wasn't going to say a thing, and then I looked over at Kyle. "The authorities have been notified." I watched his expression.

He looked delighted. "Good. Because after I heard about Jason, I'd decided I was going to call Sheriff Kimball no matter what anyone said. I felt we'd been dragging our feet too long. J.B. has always put a very high price on privacy, and I do, too, but I didn't feel this was the time to worry about it." He looked over at Michael. "Were those guys who put the bugs on the phones friends of yours?"

Michael grinned. "Yes and no. The law did it." He spoke softly.

Kyle let a slow grin form on his lips. "You know, Michael, I have never believed you're the wheeler-dealer some think you are, just as I knew I wasn't the bum everyone thought I was. I'd like a peek into your own secret life someday." He stood up. "Let me know if I can be of any help." He bowed slightly in my direction. "At your service for anything you may need, beautiful lady." He sobered and picked up my hand and squeezed it. "Be careful, Laura, and good luck."

"I will be careful, Kyle, and thanks. I may need a little luck."

Mrs. Kiley offered to fix us a light dinner, but I didn't think my nerves could handle it. Michael settled for a sandwich, and we then were ready to leave. So no one would know he was going to go with me, we were going through the motions of parting. He was telling me to be careful, and I told him I would be. I felt a little foolish, since there was no one around, but if we were being watched, we made it look real.

He even took me in his arms and kissed me. I liked that touch. "Remember, when this is over, you're mine," he said softly in my ear. I reared back and looked up at him. He smiled and added, "At least, you can be sure I'm yours."

Our embrace was broken by Mrs. Kiley, who told me Harvey wanted to speak to me on the phone.

Harvey sounded agitated, as usual. "Laura, I've been thinking about your leaving those specs out there in the middle of nowhere. I just can't believe it's the only thing that can be done to get Jason back. You could leave a note and offer money, or you could—"

I cut him off. His breathing was so heavy, I worried about him for just a second. "Harvey, I don't think a note will do it. I think it's a little late to come up with Plan B. I'm getting ready to leave the ranch now."

"Now, Laura, just listen."

I listened to a long lecture about what it would do to let loose of those specs. I was getting so tired of hearing and talking about them, I almost wanted to burn them. Something had woun .arvey up, because he went on and on and on. His insistence on putting Kincade Industries first at any price seemed a little ridiculous when one realized his own nephew could be in serious danger. Maybe, since he had no family of his own, Kincade Industries *was* his family.

When I realized this was going to be one of those endless speeches by Harvey, I cut him off again. "Harvey, I won't make it out to Cutter Hill by nine o'clock if I don't leave now. I'll call you when I get back."

"Uh, Laura. . . ." His tone changed, and he hesitated just a moment. "I have to go out for a little while. I may or may not be back by the time you get out to the ranch. If I'm not here when you call, don't worry, I'll call you as soon as I get home." His words came slowly, as though he were thinking as he spoke. It wasn't like Harvey. It was generally thought Harvey spoke first and thought afterward.

"Okay, Harvey, good-bye." I hung up.

I looked out in the foyer, and Michael was gone. He was going to fit himself either on the floor of the backseat or in the trunk. It would be a tight fit either way for someone with his long legs. I picked up my bag and that infernal envelope and left my office. Kyle was coming down the stairs. I had a flash of an idea. I didn't know what it meant, but Kyle would be a good source of information if it did no more good than take care of my curiosity. "Kyle, you said your studio is in Harvey's guest house. I gather he doesn't have many guests."

"No, not many since his wife left him eight or nine years ago." He gave me a curious look. "Whatever I know is yours, beautiful. Harvey has a big house, so he can put up a few people when he wants to. He has someone there now. When I went by this noon to pick up my paintings, I heard the stereo going in the house, and the kitchen window was open. Harvey locks up tight when he goes to the office. It's not the day for his cleaning lady. And it wasn't Harvey's type of music. He probably has one of the finest stereo and sound systems there is. It's his hobby, you know. He loves tinkering with speakers and what-all. He tells me about it, but I never know what he's talking about."

It seemed a curious hobby for Harvey, with his own short fuse. I didn't really know why I cared. "Was there a strange car around?"

"You're turning into quite a detective, aren't you? I didn't see a car around, so someone probably flew in. He's had a few friends from the East who have come out lately. I'd say this is the third or fourth. I don't pry into his business and, thankfully, he doesn't pry into mine."

Kyle wished me luck again, and I left the house.

At the garage I got into J.B.'s big Lincoln, adjusted the seat and mirror, fastened my seat belt, and took several deep breaths. My heart was racing, my palms were damp, and my stomach was churning. I told myself that all I had to do was a simple delivery job. I started the car and let it run for a minute.

Barney Tully came up to the window. "Laura, I

don't like this a bit. I don't like your going out there at this time of night."

I took another breath. "The only ones who like the idea are Jason's kidnappers. I'll be careful, really."

"Well, you just remember—you got a lot of power under that hood. You get scared or anything, you just lay down on that accelerator, and this baby will move for you." He leaned inside the car farther and lowered his voice. He moved one hand around, as though he were telling me about the car. "Michael is in the trunk. We have the latch fixed so he can get out in a hurry if he has to. If the drop is uneventful, stop as soon as you're well away from the drop sight so he can get out. He'll be mighty cramped." He pulled his head back out of the window and spoke in a more normal voice. "You be careful now, you hear?"

I smiled. "I will, Barney." I raised the window, moved the car out of the driveway, and drove out the lane to the highway. It was the biggest car I'd ever driven. I turned east on Highway 50 and started the climb up the mountain.

Suddenly, in the middle of the anxiety attack I was sure I was having, it came to me where I had seen those three company names that seemed familiar. They had made bids on the Whitaker project I had worked on with J.B. some time ago. They were research and development firms. My stomach sank. I didn't want to think about why Jason had their phone numbers in his apartment.

I turned my mind to something Kyle had said: "Harvey has a house guest." So what? I let that roll around in my mind for a while to keep myself from thinking about where I was going. I wished we had some assurance that Jason was all right. Why hadn't Michael insisted on it?

I knew I was getting close to my turnoff. A sign for Cutter Hill showed up in my headlights. I made my turn onto the off ramp and continued on a narrow road until I came to the first dirt road on the right. I turned into it slowly, thinking of Michael in the trunk. My headlights picked up nothing but a maze of tall pines and a road that looked like little more than a narrow tunnel through the trees. I checked my odometer and drove the prescribed two miles, with a death grip on the steering wheel.

CHAPTER ELEVEN

WHEN the odometer said I'd gone two miles, I stopped the car. The trees surrounded me like dark, eerie sentinels. It was a pitch-black night. With my heart beating loudly in my ears and my knees feeling like they were filled with jelly, I picked up the envelope and opened the door. With more effort than it had ever taken before, I stepped out of the car.

I stood up and leaned against the car for support while I sucked in more air than I needed. My hands were trembling, my skin felt cold, and I prayed I wouldn't become paralyzed by fear. The red box the caller had mentioned sat at the base of a tree in front of me. Putting one foot in front of the other, breathing in ragged spurts, I made my way over the deep bed of pine needles. The knowledge that Michael lay waiting for a call of distress from me, and knowing I might be helping Jason, gave me the whisper of courage I needed to proceed.

I reached the box and turned around. I felt painfully alone, but I knew better. I was sure I was being watched. The goose bumps on my arms told me that.

I opened the lid of the box. A note was taped to the inside of the lid. It wasn't easy to read in the headlights, but I worked at it, thinking it might have further instructions. My hands trembled even more when I recognized the writing.

Laura,

I'm all right. If you leave the right specs, I'll be home tomorrow night, I'm told. I think we can believe them. I'm grateful you were willing to do this. If anyone but you makes this drop, I'm in deep trouble. Get out of here fast. They're watching you.

Love,
Jason

I dropped the specs into the box, closed the lid, and ran back to the car. I got in and hit the button that locked all the doors. Because of the small, open area, and because I wasn't used to manipulating such a big car, and because my nerves marred my judgment so badly, I had difficulty turning around to get out of there. When I finally did get that accomplished, I drove out of the area slowly so as not to jar Michael too much. Had I been alone, I know I would have raced over that rough road with little regard for the consequences to the car.

When I turned onto the highway again, I let out a long breath, but I had difficulty making my hands stop shaking. I drove about four miles before I spotted a turnout space wide enough for me to pull off.

I jumped out of the car and ran to the trunk to release Michael.

When I reached the trunk, since it was set up so Michael could release it, I spoke out loud. "Okay, Michael, you can get out now. We're away from there, and there was no problem."

When I received no answer and nothing happened, I rapped on the trunk and repeated myself. When I still received no answer, my heart raced again, and I inserted the key and gave it a sharp turn. The hood popped up. I gasped and grabbed the fender for support. The trunk was empty.

CHAPTER TWELVE

I SLAMMED the trunk closed and ran to the side of the car. I opened the driver's door and peered at the backseat and then down at the floor. There was no sign of Michael. I looked around at the pitch-black that surrounded me. Down the road behind me, pinheads of lights told me a vehicle was coming toward me. I jumped into the car and locked the doors again. The car slowed and stopped beside me. It was a van, and the passenger put the window down. I opened mine. "Are you all right, lady?" the man asked.

I nodded. "Yes, thank you. I'm ready to leave now."

He drove on slowly. I bit my lip and waited for a minute. *Michael, where are you? When did you get out?* He had to be back there where I left the specs. Should I have waited for him? How would he get out of there? What would happen to him if *they* found him?

I eased back onto the road with my mind whirling in every direction, searching for answers, for the course of action I should take. The van that had stopped beside me was pulled off to the side of the road. After I passed, it eased onto the road behind me. My hands started to shake again.

The traffic was light on the highway, but I drew some comfort from the other cars. That van stayed with me. My heart pounded in my ears. I was approaching the turnoff for the ranch. My hope was that the van would continue on and prove to me my imagination was out of control.

I put on my turn signal and took the off ramp. I was relieved to see the van didn't turn on its turn signal. I was on the off ramp when the van made a sharp turn and came up behind me.

I came to an intersection and stopped. The van stopped behind me. There wasn't a building in sight. Going one way, it was twenty-five miles to the ranch, but the other way it was only about ten miles to Harvey's house. As much as I'd dislike asking the man's help or advice, I felt the need to talk to someone who should care about what happened to Michael and Jason. I also needed to go somewhere where I could get off the road and away from the van behind me.

I turned toward Harvey's house. Normally I loved the country, but alone at night, with no sign of life except that van behind me and not a streetlight to be seen, it was intimidating. I hit the steering wheel, regretting my turn toward Harvey's. He wasn't what I considered a reasonable man. Maybe Kyle would be at his studio. Maybe. I idly wondered who Harvey's house guest might be. If it was a woman, my presence might not be welcomed. Too bad!

When I turned into the street where Harvey lived, the van went straight ahead. That, in itself, helped my nervous condition. I had been to Harvey's house only once, over a year before, when I had delivered some papers there while he was recovering from minor surgery with all the drama of a Greek tragedy.

I remembered his house sat back from the road some distance. It was distinctive, but it wasn't easy picking out his rambling structure from other rambling structures nearly hidden by the trees. I passed Harvey's house before I realized it. The houses were spaced quite a distance from one another, and each sat on a sizable piece of land.

I drove down the narrow street until I found a place where I could safely pull the car off the road. There were no sidewalks in that area, and the trees and scrub growth lined the narrow road right up to the hard surface. Moving a big car around in a small space is not an inborn talent, and I didn't care to try backing up to Harvey's house. I walked back to Harvey's house and, for some reason, felt relieved that there were no lights on there.

I walked to the side of the house and opened the gate. Then I spotted the guest house. It sat a long way in back of the house, barely visible from the main house. It, too, was dark. Again I hesitated, wondering what to do. *Michael, Michael, where are you?* I turned around and decided I'd better find a phone and call Sheriff Kimball and tell him what had happened.

As I walked toward the front of the house, a car pulled into the driveway. I stepped back behind a big oak tree and waited. Off to the side, well in my view, the garage door opened by remote control. Harvey's car drove in. He stepped out of the car, and I could have sworn he was smiling. One thing Harvey Kincade rarely did was smile.

He reached into the car and took out a large manila envelope that matched the one I had just left in the woods. He slammed the door. My chest tightened, and I had to stifle a scream of anger.

I couldn't move for a minute. My mind froze. Harvey, of all people—the man whose litany about loyalty and integrity being the true signs of what a man or woman is worth was burned into the memory of every Kincade Industries employee for eternity. This same Harvey had kidnapped his own nephew and stolen the company's most valuable asset at the moment.

I scooted along the side of the house, running between some tall pine trees. Somehow I made my way back to J.B.'s car. I remembered a gas station no more than a mile or so down the road. It was closed, but there was a light by the phone booth. The van that had followed me flickered through my mind, but I ignored it.

I called Sheriff Kimball. He was out, but I left a message telling him I knew who picked up the specs and where he was. I also tried to tell about Michael in as few words as possible. I wasn't sure the person I was talking to didn't think I might possibly have taken leave of my senses, but he said he'd get the message to Sheriff Kimball as soon as possible.

I then called the ranch and told Mrs. Kiley that if Michael called to tell him I was at Harvey's. I told her to alert everyone in the house, but I didn't tell her more. I didn't feel up to it. I assured her I was fine and that the drop went without incident. Of course, I didn't mention that Michael and I had gotten separated. No one but Barney knew he left with me. Or did he leave with me?

Just as I was getting back into the car, the van showed up. "Hey, pretty lady, want to party?" One of the men in it opened the door and stepped out.

I leaped into the car, locked the doors, started the engine, and did as Barney Tully told me. I stepped down hard on the accelerator. I undoubtedly left some rubber on the driveway. But Barney was right. That car could move. I probably broke every law in the driving code, but when I turned into Harvey's street once again, the van was not behind me. When I arrived at Harvey's house this time, I pulled into the driveway.

Filled with bravado, I couldn't wait to face Harvey, find out where Jason was being held and just what might have happened to Michael. I was secure with the fact that Sheriff Kimball would be along very soon. I was also secure with the thought that I could handle Harvey. He was short and fat and terribly out of condition. I pressed down on the doorbell until Harvey opened the door.

"Hey, you knew. . . ." It was a moment to be remembered in history. Harvey Kincade was at a loss for words. "Laura," he finally said as though in shock, which undoubtedly did describe his condition quite well, "Laura, what are you—"

I cut him off. "I'm here, Harvey, because I saw you walk into the house carrying the manila envelope I left for the men who have kidnapped Jason."

I pushed him back into the house and closed the door. His eyes darted to the desk in the corner of the room. The envelope was on top. I walked over and picked it up.

"Now," I said with great confidence, "you'll tell me where you have Jason stashed. You are such a contemptible man to use your own nephew and steal from your own family's firm."

He sank into a big chair. "Laura," he said softly, "you don't understand."

I stood before him and glared down at him. "Why don't you explain it to me, Harvey? Maybe, just maybe, I might understand. Most people think I'm quite bright, you know." I watched his face flush and tears come from his eyes. I couldn't believe what I was seeing.

He started slowly. "Oh, Laura, it's because you're so young and so pretty and so bright that you may not be able to understand." He drew in a deep breath. "You know how J.B. and Father treat me. I've been the family buffoon all my life. I'm fifty-seven years old, and I've always wanted to get even with them, pay them back. Our company policy says I have to retire in five years, and I wasn't sure I'd ever get another chance to hurt them like the loss of the Hardcase project would."

He wasn't talking to me as much as he was talking to himself. He was a pathetic sight as he looked off at the wall on the other side of the room. "Did you have to use your own nephew?" I knew he wouldn't answer that, if he heard it. "Go on, Harvey."

"I saw it as my last chance." He looked up at me. "I could have done this easier if you people hadn't set up that office at the ranch. I could move freer at the office, get to people better. I could have handled all this in a much simpler way. Through your computer I knew you'd know every copy that might be made of the specs. Of course, you'd expect to know who and why. At the office I could have covered myself so much better. There, no one would question my judgment, but I knew you would out there when you had little else to do except monitor the Hardcase project and everything concerning it."

He took in a deep breath. "But, of course, no one has ever listened to me. I pushed Jason. I made him go through all your papers in your office at the ranch. I needed to know everything you had out there. J.B. wouldn't tell me. For once I think Jason was a little in awe of me. He's never been that way before. I reminded him I could be running Kincade Industries if J.B. didn't recover. Do you understand, Laura?"

The tears and the look on his face blew away some of my bravado. I walked over to the fireplace and opened the envelope. "Where are you holding Jason? Who's in this with you?" I pulled out the papers from the envelope, and my mouth dropped open. "Harvey, these are blank sheets of paper!"

Harvey's body jerked forward. "That can't be!" He held out his hand, and I gave him the papers. "It can't be. . . ." His voice trailed off. "He went to the box, picked up the envelope, and brought it back to me. You. . . ." He glared accusingly at me.

"Harvey, the specs were in the envelope I left in the box. I haven't let that thing out of my sight, hardly out of my hand, since you gave it to me this afternoon. I even sat on it at times. I'm not the one who has pulled this on you. It's whoever picked up the envelope. Who is it, Harvey?"

I waited for him to answer, but he only stared at the blank sheets of paper. He mumbled something about not appreciating something, but I couldn't understand him. His eyes became glassy, and I filled with panic.

"Harvey," I yelled, "where is Jason? Who helped you with this?"

He looked up at me blankly for just a moment before he placed his hand on his chest. "He'll be home. . . ." He slumped in the chair.

I ran to his side and yelled again. "Harvey, speak to me! Harvey—"

His eyes rolled up, and his lids dropped. He slumped farther down in the chair.

I ran to the phone and called 911. I yelled at the man who answered, but tried my best to speak concisely when I told him where to send an ambulance.

I wasn't sure what to do while I waited. I willed the sheriff to knock on the door. I loosened Harvey's tie, opened his shirt, and placed a cold, wet facecloth on his forehead. He'd groan once in a while, and he mumbled something inaudible. I kept assuring him help was on the way.

When a car drove in the driveway, I ran to the door and threw it open. Sheriff Kimball stepped in, frowning. "You should have waited for me, Miss Grant." He looked at Harvey. "What happened?"

"I don't know," I told him, "but I think he's having a heart attack. I've called for an ambulance." While the sheriff and the man in plain clothes who stepped into the house behind him tended to Harvey, I went into the kitchen and took several deep breaths and let them out slowly.

Thankfully, the paramedics arrived and went to work on Harvey. In no time they had him ready to transport. As the men carried Harvey out to the ambulance, a young doctor stepped into the kitchen. "Miss, Mr. Kincade just said, 'Tell her he'd be home.' Does that make sense to you?"

I thought for a minute. He must have meant Jason. "Yes, I think so. Thank you, doctor. Has he had a heart attack?"

"It looks like it."

"Does it look . . . fatal?"

He shrugged. "Hard to tell. We'll know more later."

After he left, I joined the sheriff in the living room. I told him what I knew. "I can't believe this," I said.

Sheriff Kimball, a tall, solid man in his early forties, laid his hand on my shoulder. "It's always hard to accept it when people we know go wrong." He turned to the man beside him. "Miss Grant, this is Agent Bidwell from the FBI."

I nodded. He was the one Michael called Frank. At another time I'd have bombarded the man with questions about Michael, but, of course, the time was wrong. "Did you understand my message about Michael, sheriff?"

"Yes, I did. I gather he got out of the trunk at the drop sight."

I nodded. "Is someone out looking for him?" I asked.

"Yes, and there are two FBI men who were out there who haven't been heard from, either," he said.

I shuddered. Another car arrived. Two plain-clothesmen came into the house. "We just heard from Murdock," one man told Agent Bidwell. "He and Hutch are all right. They got a license number for us, but they also got bushwacked and hit on the head. They were out about twenty minutes, as close as Murdock can tell. Michael Kincade is with them. We told them to come here."

I let out a loud sigh of relief. Sheriff Kimball smiled.

I tried to sit still while we waited for Michael and the two FBI men to arrive. I also tried to figure out who Harvey's accomplice might be. With the specs missing and Harvey's unknown accomplice apparently pulling the old double cross, I had the feeling we were back to square one.

A half hour later Michael walked in the door with two other men. They all looked the worse for wear.

I ran into Michael's arms. "Oh, Michael, I was so worried about you!"

He kissed me lightly. "I didn't want to tell you what I'd planned, because I knew you'd only give me a lot of chatter about it. See, I'm all right."

I stepped back, indignant. I brushed at the dirt on his windbreaker. "Well, you're a mess, and I bet you have a gigantic headache." I couldn't stay indignant. I became angry. "You could have been killed."

Sheriff Kimball spoke up. "So could you, miss. You shouldn't have come here by yourself. Harvey could have had a gun, or he could have had someone here who had one. He was perfectly in the clear as far as I know and, at that time, you were the only one who could accuse him."

"Of course, you're right, sheriff. Somehow I guess I never thought of Harvey as being a physically dangerous man, no matter what I knew he'd done." I shrugged guiltily. "And I never thought of the possibility of anyone else being here." I looked up at him. "The house was dark."

Sheriff Kimball frowned. "That doesn't necessarily mean a house is empty."

"Of course." Properly chastised, I remained quiet while Agent Bidwell and the sheriff filled in Michael and the other two agents. I added a couple of details of Harvey's dialogue, and then I had a thought. "Kyle told me Harvey likes to fool around with sound systems and his stereo and such. I bet he'd know how to make those tapes and distort the voices."

Agent Murdock held up two tapes. "These may be the ones." He walked over to a tape deck with the two tapes he had picked up from the desk. When he turned on the tape deck, we heard a repeat of our two recorded phone calls.

I looked up at Michael. "I'd like to go to Jason's apartment and wait for him," I said. "He'll be able to tell us just who is involved in all this besides Harvey."

"I'll go with you," he said. He talked to the two agents and the sheriff for a few minutes, and then we left. I hoped he'd open the door to Jason's apartment again so we could wait inside. The packing of the suitcase and the scent of shaving lotion still bothered me. It would, somehow, have been in character for Harvey to have tried out the shaving lotion, but it couldn't have been him. We knew he had been at the office all morning.

Michael offered to drive to Jason's apartment, and I was willing to let him. I had no desire to take that car into city traffic. On the way, I watched Michael for a few minutes. He was deep in thought. When I spoke, I measured my words. "Michael, you told me you'd tell me all when this case was all cleared up. Do I have to wait until the bitter end, or will you tell me now just who Michael Kincade might be?"

He glanced over at me and grinned. He picked up one of my hands and squeezed it. "You don't let up, do you? Believe me, Michael Kincade is no big thing. Because I've never told anyone here at home, my existence is made to seem that way. After I got my law degree at Stanford, my father was insistent that I go to work for Kincade Industries, of course. I wanted no part of it. It was part of the reason I worked most of the time I was going to college. I wanted to pay my way as much as I could while I got my education, so I wouldn't feel obligated."

He looked ahead of him. I thought I'd heard a touch of anger in his voice. "That doesn't bother most kids," I said.

"Well, it did me. I knew my education was for Kincade Industries as much as for me. Anyway, Father wouldn't let up. Then he tried to get me to go to work at Uncle Teddy's bank. He could see no reason why I should choose my own occupation when my family and ancestors had set up opportunities for me."

"So what did you do?" I spoke softly. As much as I was bursting to know, I didn't want to push him too hard.

"You can imagine what a donnybrook we had. Anyway, I went East, and to make a long story short, I ended up in Washington, D.C." He looked over at me and grinned. I relaxed a little. "I've worked for the Diplomatic Corps for almost ten years. Actually, I carry the title of Aide to Ambassadors. I've worked for many of them. I'm usually sent in if there's a hint of trouble. I keep my ear to the ground and my eyes open. Sometimes, because of the access my status allows me, I can find out things the CIA knows but can't nail down. We, of course, keep them informed. Sometimes I can get verification of things for them."

I scowled. "It sounds fascinating and exciting, but

also a dangerous way to live." I couldn't believe how relieved I felt. I'd given up thoughts that he might be outside the law when I knew he'd called in the FBI, but I'd still had a few doubts about just where he might stand. Of course, I should have known better, I told myself.

"There've been a few close calls, and I did get hurt a couple of times, but it's not like the CIA can be at times. I almost joined them, but I took the offer of the Diplomatic Corps because I felt I'd have a little more freedom and I was better qualified."

"You could have told your family, you know. For a while, after you left home, they probably worried about you."

Bright lights started to light our way as we traveled the last leg of our trip down into the valley and the city. Michael laughed. "By the time I left, I'm not sure they were worried so much as they were eaten up with curiosity. I really think they thought I couldn't make it without the family name behind me. No one else in recent generations has ever tried."

"You were brave to try it."

"Anyway, after I started to travel, it was a game I played, I guess, not to tell them what I was doing. Childish on my part, I know, but it gave me a little satisfaction. I made it a point to call home every couple of months to make sure everyone was all right. More often than not, I talked to Mrs. Kiley. She'd just tell me about everyone and ask how I was doing, and we'd let it go at that. I'd send cards or notes when

I was transferred, just to let them know my where-abouts at the moment.

"Dad and Jason used to demand I tell them what I do, told me it was my duty to tell them, and after a while, when I wouldn't give them a straight answer, they probably thought the worst." He laughed again. "My ego can handle that. Kyle has asked a couple of times, but he did it more honestly than the rest. He told me he was just nosy."

"I can see why you didn't get a bigger reception when you arrived."

"Hey, it was one of the better ones this time. My father has never forgiven me for the fact that I haven't needed his help. Mother told me when I left home that she knew I could take care of myself and she wanted me to enjoy life. I think of that often. She's always had a phone number in Washington that she could call and leave a message for me. She wanted Mrs. Kiley to have it, too, but no one else knows about it. She used it for the first time when Father had his first stroke. When I come home, she always acts as though I've been away for the weekend."

We pulled into the parking lot at Jason's apartment house. I couldn't believe how much better I felt. He shut off the engine and turned to face me. He picked up my hand and went on. "About six months ago I was shot in the side. I spent some time in the hospital and used that time to think about my life. I realized I'd had more adventure and excitement and glamour in my life than most men dream of or that any sane man would want. I decided it was time I settled down. The first thing I did was put in for a job in the legal department of the FBI. Next I tried to decide how a man knows when he's met the one right woman for him. When I met you, my question was answered."

I couldn't breathe. "Michael—"

I was interrupted by a man knocking on the window of the car door.

"Everything all right here?" the security guard asked.

I wanted to say I didn't know, but Michael nodded and opened the door. "We're here visiting my brother, Jason Kincade."

"Yes, sir, Mr. Kincade. He's probably in. I just passed his car back there. It's a beauty."

We got out of the car and walked across the parking lot. Just as we reached the door to the building, we looked at each other and burst out laughing. I'm not sure what he was thinking, but I felt like a teenager who had just been caught necking on lovers' lane.

Michael held the door for me, and when he stopped laughing, he spoke softly. "We'll continue our conversation later."

I looked up at him. "I certainly hope so."

CHAPTER THIRTEEN

WHEN we reached Jason's apartment, Michael prepared to get the lock open again. "Is that what the Diplomatic Corps teaches you?"

He grinned. "Hardly. In fact, it's one of my talents they might frown on."

He bent down, and I thought I heard a sound from inside. I touched his shoulder. "Listen—I think I hear something."

He put his ear to the door and looked up at me. "I hear it too."

Michael stood up and pushed the doorbell. Jason opened the door, wearing a big grin until he saw us. "Laura . . . Michael. . . ." His jaw dropped. We were definitely not who he expected.

Without thinking, I threw my arms around him. "Oh, Jason, I was so worried about you!"

He put his hands on my sides, but I had the feeling he wasn't being affectionate. I stepped back. Michael walked briskly by him. "Glad you're all right, Jason," he said. "You have a lot of information we need, and the quicker you can give it to us, the better for everyone. By the way, Harvey's had a heart attack. He's in the hospital."

I cannot imagine a more shocked and perplexed expression than on Jason's face. I stepped into his apartment and closed the door.

When he regained his voice, Jason laughed lightly. "Hey, you two. Slow down. Tell me what's going on here. What's this about Harvey?"

Michael turned around and faced Jason. "We'll tell you what we know as soon as you tell us what you know. Who was in this with Harvey? Where can we find him? What are his plans? He switched the specs on Harvey and gave him an envelope filled with plain white papers."

Jason staggered backward. "Well, I . . . don't. . . ." His voice failed him, and he hesitated.

An idea was fighting for recognition in my mind. I frowned at it, but it kept struggling.

The two brothers stood looking at each other. To me, it looked as though Michael had the advantage since he had his hand on his hips and his gaze was direct. His eyes didn't blink. Jason, on the other hand, at a loss for words, blinked his eyes continually and struggled to regain his poise.

"Well?" Michael said sternly.

Michael would have intimidated me if he'd glared at me like that and spoken so sharply. I had the feeling Jason was intimidated too, but he held his ground, groping for words. I could see his demeanor returning to normal. I wondered what his problem might be. I wondered if he'd do better without me there . . . if there was something he'd rather I didn't know since Harvey was involved.

And then that idea that had only flickered around in my mind a few moments ago burst into full bloom. "Excuse me, guys. I'm going to freshen up." I turned and walked toward Jason's bedroom.

Jason came to life. "Laura, no—use the guest-room bath."

I wondered if he knew he shouted at me. But it was too late. I was standing in the doorway to his bedroom, and there on the bed was a large manila envelope. I called to Michael as I walked over to the bed and picked up the envelope. I opened it slowly, and inside were the specifications for the Hardcase project.

Jason looked at Michael. His whole body sagged as he let out a long breath. "Okay, Michael, your brains and your guts got you out." His voice was filled with despair. "The sale of this was going to get me out of debt and be my ticket for a new start in New York, where I had the guarantee of a job at a lot better salary than Father pays me." Michael picked up the phone, and Jason looked at him almost sadly. "Michael, tell me how you got out and were able to stay out. What do you do?"

I thought the phrase *got out* was an odd one, but I knew he meant out from under the Kincade world. Michael's glance at his brother was touched with understanding, I thought. He looked over at me and then back at Jason. "I'll tell you about it while we wait for the FBI."

*   *   *

It was over. It was two o'clock in the morning. I was starving. We had a long drive back to the ranch. I got into the car and caught my foot on the rubber floor mat that covered the lush carpet. I bent down to move it back into place and felt something. Raising the mat again, I uncovered a large manila envelope. Inside was the copy of the specs Michael and I had torn the ranch apart to find.

Michael hit the steering wheel. "That's my father. No one but him drives this car. Not even Barney. It's been sitting in the garage locked up since Father had his first stroke, except for the night we took him to the hospital. Under normal circumstances no one would have taken this car from the garage until he could drive again."

I put the envelope back under the mat. "It's been safe there all this time; it should be safe there a little longer," I said. For just a moment raging fury rose in me, but it quickly subsided. Everything was over now, and being angry wasn't going to help anything. "I didn't eat dinner. Can we get something to eat before I faint?"

Michael looked over at me and grinned. "I think we can work it out."

Most of my questions had been answered except one. "Michael, did Jason tell you, when I was out of the room, why he switched the envelopes on Harvey? Was he just going to split and leave Harvey?"

Michael's jaw tightened. "It seems Harvey had a buyer lined up for the specs, but Jason found someone willing to pay a whole lot more and give him that job he talked about. They've been working on this ever since the deal was set up for Kincade Industries to do the research and development for Watson & Company. How long has that been?"

"About eight or nine months, I guess."

"Anyway, Harvey wouldn't give in and back out of the first deal he made. Harvey has a funny kind of loyalty, I guess. He told Jason his word was his bond." He looked over at me and grinned. "Who can figure some people's logic? Anyway, Jason wanted to secure his future with the buyer he'd found. He intended to split the cash he got for the specs with Harvey, then leave for New York in a month or so. Jason wanted to just walk away the way I did, he said."

"What will happen to Jason and Harvey now?"

"I don't know. It'll depend on what charges my father will want to file against them. I think Gramps would hang them, but I'm not too sure that Father won't merely be willing to settle for banishing them from the ranch, Kincade Industries, the state, and the country, if he can. I'd like to wait a while before we tell him. He'd probably have another stroke."

I thought of the raging wrath J.B. was capable of displaying and shuddered. I tried to ignore what I knew about his bad investment. Poor J.B. When he regained his health to a degree, he wouldn't be greeted with good news. "You know he's going to want to know everything that's been going on." I shuddered again. "I hate to admit it, Michael, but I've had a few lingering doubts about Amanda. Now

I think she's the only one in your family who is what she seems to be."

He chuckled as he pulled into the parking lot of an all-night coffee shop. "Gramps once called her an overeducated spoiled brat. I guess he hit it pretty close. I keep hoping she'll grow up, but she's twenty-eight, and I don't see it starting yet. With Amanda, what you see is all there is."

While I looked over the menu, Michael went to the phone booth. He came back and joined me, looking pleased. "Uncle Harvey is holding his own, and the prognosis is good. My father had a good day. They think he'll be out of intensive care within the next couple of days. His left arm may be partially paralyzed, but that's all they see now. That means he's lucky. We'll go see him tomorrow and tell him about the new life we'll be starting soon."

I looked up at him, and my eyebrows shot up. "Oh?"

"Murdock told me tonight that my request for a job in the legal department of the FBI has gone through. I can start the first of the month. My two choices for assignment were Sacramento and San Francisco." His smile was smug. "I lucked out. I can have my choice. There's an opening in both offices. Think about it, sweetheart. I told Murdock I'd let him know tomorrow which post we'd take."

He didn't have to say more. The waitress came and asked us what we wanted. At that moment I had everything I wanted.